A DIRTY WEDDING NIGHT

JAINE DIAMOND

DREAM WARP BOOKS

A Dirty Wedding Night
Jaine Diamond

Published by DreamWarp Publishing Ltd.
www.jainediamond.com

Cover Design: DreamWarp Publishing Ltd.

Join Jaine's **Diamond Club Newsletter** to get free bonus content, new release info, giveaways and insider updates.

A Dirty Wedding Night

For every reader who wanted more…

Author's Note

In *Dirty Like Brody*, we get to attend Jesse and Katie's rock star wedding—from the point of view of Brody (Dirty's longtime manager) and Jessa (Jesse's sister and former Dirty songwriter).

This book, *A Dirty Wedding Night*, is a four-story collection about what happens between Jesse and Katie on their wedding night… and three other couples who secretly hook up that night!

The four stories in *A Dirty Wedding Night* are somewhat interwoven, and are meant to be read in order.

With love from the beautiful west coast of Canada (the home of Dirty!),
Jaine

A Dirty Vow

Author's Note

Jesse and Katie's love story begins in *Dirty Like Me*, and in that book, they get their happily-ever-after ending... yet it's not really an ending. It's just the beginning of their lives together.

In *Dirty Like Brody*, we get to attend Jesse and Katie's rock star wedding at a remote luxury resort called Cathedral Cove, on the Canadian Pacific Coast.

In that book, Jesse and Katie's wedding night—*after* the wedding reception—ends with Jesse's band, Dirty, having drinks and a musical jam with a few close friends around an outdoor fire pit. We get to experience the jam, which stretches into the wee hours, from band manager Brody's point of view.

As the jam finally winds down and some of the remaining party-goers opt to take an impromptu skinny dip in the frigid waters of the cove, Jesse and Katie have vanished. Obviously, the newly-weds have headed off to their luxurious cabin for wedding night sex, right?

In this story, we get a glimpse of the relationship politics around the fire pit from Jesse's point of view. Then… we get to find out what happens when Jesse and Katie finally get to celebrate their wedding night—alone.

Or maybe not so alone…?

Though there's plenty of sex in Jesse and Katie's book, *Dirty Like Me*, there are actually no sex scenes from Jesse's point of view. In *A Dirty Vow*, we get that, and more.

So, for all of you who've asked for MORE of Jesse and Katie, even after they got their happily ever after (and thank you for that!)… this one's for you, with love.

Jaine

Chapter One

Jesse

The fire bathed Katie's face in lapping, golden light. She was sitting right beside me and she was so fucking beautiful, with her creamy skin and her sweet features and her dark hair... she laughed at something Zane said, and my stomach twirled.

Butterflies. The girl actually gave me butterflies.

As she raised her champagne glass to her lips, gazing into the fire, I glimpsed the platinum wedding band I'd slipped onto her finger earlier this evening; it glinted in the dark, reflecting the flames, and it gave me a total rush. That shiny band now marked Katie Bloom as married. As *mine*.

And that shit was making me hard.

Her cheeks and the tip of her nose were rosy; it was cold out, but that flush might've been from the booze. She was definitely a little drunk, but it was a cute drunk. She'd been pacing herself throughout the night. I'd made sure of that. Because sometimes when Katie got too drunk, she couldn't come, and that wouldn't fucking do.

Not on our wedding night.

Not when I was desperate to watch her come; to *feel* her come.

Several times.

She caught me perving on her and smiled. Her big blue-green eyes widened in the firelight—and that sweetly surprised look went straight to my cock. Just like it always did.

Didn't exactly help matters that she hadn't let me fuck her in two long, aching days.

Save it for our wedding night, she'd said, fending off my wandering hands as we arrived here at the resort, on the morning of the wedding rehearsal. *It will be better if we wait.*

Which sounded like a nice idea at the time. Romantic. Hot.

But that was yesterday. Before she proceeded to dance with me, flirt with me, make out with me at her stagette party—in a super-thin bikini top and minuscule cut-offs—then make me sleep in a separate bed.

Today, she danced with me again, flirted with me some more, married me in a jaw-dropping-gorgeous dress, and at the reception, let me peel off her garter with my tongue. Without ever *once* giving my aching dick so much as a pity stroke.

If I'd known by "wedding night" she actually meant almost dawn the next morning, I would've screwed her senseless every step of the way.

Because fuck waiting.

I held her gaze, sipping my beer, my tongue playing idly with the neck of the bottle, thinking about all the shit I was gonna do to her the second I got her alone… until her smile melted into something else, her teeth catching on her plump bottom lip.

Then my gaze slid deliberately south… to the hint of cleavage and that alluring dip between her breasts, bared by her half-unzipped, down-filled jacket… to her sexy, curvy legs, crossed, in

her tight jeans…. to her furry boots. They were new, and I hadn't fucked her in them yet.

I was gonna have to remedy that. Soon.

"Jesus Christ. Quit eye-fucking your bride and go do it already."

I glanced at Zane, my lead singer and one of my groomsmen. I had to kind of blink him into focus, I was so cross-eyed with lust.

He was sitting on Katie's other side, a dirty, cocky smirk on his face. It was the one he usually used on women he was planning to fuck. Since he was using it on *me* right now, it was meant to piss me off—since his arm was around my wife.

"You know, you're married now," he went on, his fingertips grazing Katie's shoulder. "It's not a sin anymore." The touch was so light she probably didn't even feel it through her puffy jacket. But it wasn't meant for her. It was meant for me, because this was how Zane entertained himself when my woman was around. "Unless you're waiting on some pointers…?"

"Zane, don't tease," Katie scolded him, but she was still smiling too. She liked my friends; I liked that. She even put up with Zane's flirting, which was both cool and annoying.

"Yeah, man. The fuck are you waiting for?" Dylan chimed in. My drummer was now grinning at me across the fire.

Not good.

Zane and Dylan ganging up on me was never good. Unlike Zane, Dylan rarely busted my balls when it came to Katie… which clearly meant that us newlyweds were wearing out our welcome at the fire.

Which was totally fucking fine with me.

I'd felt a little obligated to hang out with our wedding guests, even though the reception was long over, and I knew Katie did, too. After all, they'd come all the way up here, hours north of the city, by floatplane, just to attend our wedding—at a remote resort in the wilderness that didn't even have Wi-Fi—despite the fact that many of them were rock stars, or people who worked with rock stars, and therefore had other shit to do. I figured the least we could do was keep them fed, liquored, and entertained.

Still; if I didn't get to bury my dick in my new wife soon, I was gonna explode. Maybe literally. I'd been hard all fucking day.

Well, not *all* day. But every time Katie kissed me, or brushed up against me, or looked at me like she was doing right now…

Rock hard.

I adjusted a little in my jeans, thinking about the welcoming warmth of Katie's pussy, slippery wet and swollen… all hot for me and so sweet and tight—

Jesus.

I took a cooling swig of my beer.

Time to fucking go.

Only one slight problem. That being, I didn't love leaving my little sister to the wolves.

There were only a few people left by the fire, and my sister was one of them. After the reception had wound down and most of the wedding guests stumbled off to bed, my band, Dirty, and some of our closest friends had come out to the fire pit on one of the low cliffs over the cove to jam. We'd been drinking and playing songs, which had been incredible. With my sister, Jessa, here, it was like old times. The way it used to be when we were all together and she was still with the band. The *best* times.

But now the music had died and everyone was kind of paired off and chatting. Jessa and her friend Roni were huddled together, whispering in low, conspiratorial voices, glancing over at Dylan and his buddy, Ash. I didn't even wanna know what that was about, though I was pretty sure it was about Roni, not Jessa.

Dylan and Ash were drinking and goofing around, as usual.

Brody, our band manager and another of my groomsmen, was sitting back in silence next to Maggie, our assistant manager, looking tense, just like he had the entire wedding. At least, whenever my sister was around.

And there was Zane, his arm around my wife and that infamous panty-wetting grin on his face.

"Unless, of course, you aren't up to it." Jesus; was he still fucking talking? At me? "Maybe you need a little nap? It's been a long day, and you're getting old. Pushing thirty. And you've been drinking… Maybe you just need someone to fill in for you. You know, get things warmed up—"

"That kind of comment didn't fly when I was dating her," I told him, keeping my tone casual. No way I was letting Zane fuck with me tonight, and just because he was a recovered alcoholic and therefore sober did not mean he got to win some imaginary hard dick contest. I was plenty able to fuck my wife. Didn't matter how late it got or how many beers were passed around; I'd been pacing myself, too. "It's definitely not gonna fly now that I've married her."

Zane just laughed.

Fucking guy.

I could not wait 'til he fell in love. I'd have a fucking field day with that shit. The guy was always busting everyone else's balls; he deserved some payback.

Of course, I wouldn't hold my breath waiting on Zane to get serious about a woman. Fucking around was kind of his lifeblood.

Case in point: we'd just finished jamming on an acoustic cover of "Brown Eyed Girl"—Zane's idea. He'd sung it specifically to serenade my brown-eyed sister, probably in part because he was happy she was here—we all were; it'd been fucking years since she'd been home to see us all—but also in part to piss off Brody. Because nothing ramped up Zane's meddling urges like a guy who obviously had it bad for a girl—yet failed to make a play for her.

"Hate to say it, but he's right," Brody told me, low enough

Zane wouldn't hear as he settled into a seat next to me; I was watching the cocky bastard whisper in Katie's ear, making her laugh. "Just go back to your cabin and I'll take care of things here. It's past three o'clock. At this rate, your wedding night'll be over before you consummate it."

That may have been so, but I didn't like being told when, how or where to fuck my own woman. It wasn't Brody's fault, though; he was just born bossy. Usually, I didn't mind.

"How about you?" I cocked an eyebrow at him. "Amanda?"

He sucked on his beer, looking gloomy. "Later."

I doubted that.

Brody had brought his latest "girlfriend" to the wedding, but that didn't mean much. It never did. They were always perfectly nice and perfectly pretty, with perfectly nice names like Amanda or Jennifer or Michelle—and he was always bored with them before they even got started. The odds of him actually sleeping with this one tonight seemed slim, what with the way he'd been acting around my sister all day… avoiding the shit out of her, then staring at her from afar like some lovelorn stalker.

My little sister was gorgeous; I got that. She turned heads everywhere she went, and not just because she was a lingerie model and looked like one. There was something about her that guys had always eaten up, even when she was a dorky little kid; I'd had to witness it all my life. It was this kind of awkward sweetness she had, some kind of dick-throttling magic that made boys follow her home from school and reduced grown men to idiots. Made them all—boys and men alike—want to get in her face, push her buttons; make her squeeze out a smile in their direction so they'd feel better about themselves.

None more than Brody.

I had no idea what shit had really gone down between the two of them, though what I'd once assumed was a more-or-less mutual infatuation had obviously turned south—and now neither one of them seemed able to either completely ignore or tolerate the other.

I looked at my sister across the fire. Jessa caught my eye and swiftly flashed her infamous bratty look—the one that earned her the nickname "bratface" among my friends, years ago, when they were all crushing on her but wouldn't admit it in front of me; it was the face she'd given me as a little girl when I pissed her off. I didn't even know she was still capable of that look, yet she'd been in Brody's vicinity for mere hours, and now there it was.

I didn't love it, but not much I could do. I wasn't exactly a relationship expert.

The fact that I'd managed to get Katie to the altar still kind of stunned me.

I looked at Brody. He pretended not to notice Jessa sulking and leveled me with a gray look. "Quit being a fucking hero and take your woman to bed," he muttered.

"Uh-huh." I stared at him, gauging his reaction to my words. "Guess someone should get laid tonight."

He didn't touch that. Just sipped his beer and pretended he hadn't heard me. But he still wouldn't look at my sister.

"Don't worry about it," he finally said, when he could feel me staring at him.

And I realized I didn't have to. Not really. Brody was one of the good ones. If I'd ever had qualms about the idea of any of my friends hooking up with my sister—and I did—Brody wasn't one of them. Still; if he didn't pull his head out of his ass and quit putting that bratty look on her face, I was gonna have to say something to him about it… sometime.

My wedding night, though, was not that time.

But at least one thing I knew for sure: Brody wasn't gonna let Zane or anyone else fuck with Jessa.

I sighed. "Babe," I said, standing up and extending a hand to Katie. "Let's go."

Katie beamed her sweet smile up at me, like she'd been waiting on those words all night. She took my hand and I yanked her to her feet. She fell against me, her tits squishing against my chest, just like I wanted them to.

I wrapped my arms around her waist and leaned down to give her a kiss. It was soft and slow, and earned us a bunch of whoops and growls from the guys.

So maybe I was showing off. A bit.

Then we did the obligatory round of goodnight hugs and kisses and backslaps. We got congratulated, yet again. Then I picked up my new wife and tossed her over my shoulder, despite her mild protests, and finally, we got the fuck out of there.

"Don't come back 'til she's popped your cherry!" Zane called after us as we disappeared into the dark of the trees.

"Go easy on him, Katie!" Dylan added. "He's new at this!"

And then my friends all laughed, which was understandable. They were, after all, jealous.

I couldn't blame them for that.

Chapter Two

Jesse

"I'm gonna fucking die if I can't get between your legs…"

We didn't even make it to our cabin.

I had Katie up against the railing on the wooden boardwalk that wound through the ancient trees. I could hear the waves of the cove crashing on the rocks somewhere below. I had her jeans down around her knees and I was kissing her chest, unzipping her jacket as I worked my way down. Quickly. Then I yanked her sweater up and kissed my way down her stomach.

She gasped and panted in response, clawing at my neck.

"Jesse… what if someone comes?"

"No one's coming."

That was probably true. We were on a section of the board-walk between the fire pit and the largest cabin, our cabin, and no one had a reason to come this way. Other than maybe my best friend, Jude, my best man and head of Dirty's security, who was roaming around somewhere, ever vigilant. As if some crazy paparazzo was gonna parachute into this remote resort on the

Pacific coast, way up Vancouver Island, in the middle of the night.

Well, possibly.

"We're alone," I told her as I got down on my knees and, yanking her white panties down with my fist, snaked my tongue between her legs.

"Oh… Jesse…" Katie whimpered in anticipation. She gripped my hair in fistfuls like reins, like she could hold me back, but fuck that. I was diving right in—

"Oh… *shit*."

Elle. I knew that voice, but it didn't quite compute.

My tongue froze a breath away from Katie's clit.

Elle. Dirty's bass player—and my ex-girlfriend.

"Oh—Sorry!"

That was Katie. My wife, scrabbling to cover herself, to no fucking avail, since her skinny jeans were down around her knees, tangled with her underwear.

I stood to shield her, turning around.

Elle was standing there, halfway down the stairs that led up to the wraparound deck of our cabin. It was pretty dark, but it was definitely her. Her platinum blonde hair was impossible to miss.

Maybe she didn't really see anything… but all that creamy-fair skin of Katie's under the moonlight was probably hard to miss too, even in the near-dark. And anyway, Elle wasn't an idiot.

"I was at the lookout," she said, gesturing over her shoulder.

Right… The boardwalk continued on the other side of our cabin, snaking up the cliffs to a lookout over the cove. Kinda forgot about that when I was trying to get my tongue up Katie's pussy.

"Nice up there," Elle added, awkwardly.

"Nice," I agreed. The blood wasn't exactly pumping to my brain.

"I'll… I just have to get past. To my cabin…"

"Go ahead," Katie said, clutching onto me and peeking around my shoulder. "Um… hope you had a nice night."

It was dark, but I saw Elle's gaze shift from my face to Katie's. "Yeah," she said after a moment. Then she came down the stairs and walked on by. She disappeared into the dark, without another glance in our direction.

Katie smacked my arm. "'Nice'? That's all you have to say?"

I turned back to her. "'Hope you had a nice night'?"

"Well, I do hope that."

"Katie. Any fucking way you slice it, our wedding was not nice for her."

"I know!"

"Babe." I took hold of her bare waist and softened my voice. "Don't worry about it." But I could see it already. For Katie, the moment had been ruined.

"Maybe we just… shouldn't…"

"Shouldn't? Fuck, no. Oh, fuck no." I gripped her neck and held her close, lowering my forehead to hers. "You are not putting the brakes on on our wedding night. For one thing, I'm pretty sure it's illegal."

"What?"

"We have to consummate it or the marriage isn't valid, right?"

She shrugged me off, pulling away. "I don't know. Is that even true?"

"Who cares? Let's go fuck." I caught her arm and dragged her with me toward the stairs, but she resisted.

"Jesse… don't be cold like that."

"I'm not cold, believe me. I'm burning up here."

When she dug her heels in, I turned and picked her up. I threw her over my shoulder again, pants still down.

"Jesse! Put me down."

I didn't put her down. I walked her toward the stairs, feeling my way along the handrail in the near-dark.

She slapped at my butt. "Are we seriously fighting on our wedding night?"

I set her down on the stairs and crawled over her, looking deep in her eyes. "You gonna feel guilty every time you see her because we're happy?"

"Aren't you?" Her big blue-greens blinked up at me and I softened, sighing. She sighed, too. "Okay. I'll work on it," she whispered.

"Me too." I kissed her neck.

"You'll work on feeling guilty?"

"I'll work on being more compassionate. It's hard, you know. Most of the time I'm just too damn caught up in how happy I am to give a fuck about anyone else." My hands snaked beneath her bare butt and squeezed, pulling her against me. I ground my hard dick against her for effect.

"That's not even true," she said. "I know you care about people. If you didn't, you would've hauled me off like a caveman the minute we said our vows."

"Almost did."

My lips found hers and I kissed her, softly, hungrily, the urgency building as I felt her tongue dance shyly against mine. She was holding back.

I pulled away.

"Katie, I know you have big feelings. You feel for Elle. That's part of what I love about you. But could you right now put your feelings for me and my dick ahead of those ones? We're kinda hurting over here."

I took her hand and rubbed it on my package for emphasis. Felt so fucking good… and kinda like torture. My jeans felt so tight, and they were loose fit. I couldn't remember the last time I went two days without coming.

Since before I met Katie, for sure.

"You're hurting?" she asked, giving me puppy eyes. Half-teasing, half-sympathetic.

"Fuck, yeah. I wanna make out with my wife."

She smiled. "Okay," she said softly. "Let's make out."

———

I had Katie laid out on her back on the stairs leading up to our cabin, moaning, my face between her legs and my tongue up her pussy, when I heard it.

"Jesus, get a room."

Katie jumped; actually, she totally fucking screamed.

I turned to find a big, dark-haired figure—my best friend—looming on the boardwalk, grinning down at us, a fucking smug, shit-eating grin.

I rolled over and sat up, shielding Katie again. She curled into an embarrassed ball behind me.

"You know the honeymoon suite is like ten feet in that direction?" Jude drawled, pointing up the stairs.

"Yeah," I said, in my best *go-get-fucked* tone of voice. "We're aware. What brings you by?"

"Just makin' the rounds. Thought I should make myself known when I saw you there. Otherwise, maybe I don't say anything, just slip away, but Katie opens her eyes at the last moment and sees me, thinks I'm creepin' away like some perv."

"Right. Well, appreciate it." I did, actually. "Now fuck off."

Jude laughed. Then he tipped an imaginary hat at my wife. "'Night, darlin'." Then he turned and started away into the dark.

"Goodnight, Jude!" Katie called sweetly. When he was gone, she slapped my shoulder. "Oh my God. Get me out of here!"

I grinned a little. "You embarrassed, babe?"

"Yes! Take me inside before every fucking member of your posse sees you going down on me!"

"Posse? Didn't know I had a posse…"

"You know. Your rock star posse."

"I think it's called an entourage."

"Whatever. They don't need to see your face between my legs. Let's go."

She was trying to get up the stairs with her pants down and simultaneously pull them up. I rushed her instead, picking her up. I carried her over the threshold, into our huge, luxury cabin, newlywed-style.

Then I laid her out on the dining table.

She looked like an offering to some primitive love god, sprawled there all tussled and sexy on that big slab of wood, her pants around her knees. There was a giant, three-tiered deer antler chandelier glittering above her, dappling her with light.

"What?" she asked, a little breathless.

"Just want to remember this moment," I said, admiring her.

"So remember it later as the moment you got laid." She reached to paw at me, catching a belt loop and yanking me closer. "Don't make me wait anymore."

"Me? You're the one who inflicted this bullshit waiting torture on us both."

"Whatever," she said, climbing her way up my shirt and stripping off my jacket. "So punish me."

Before she could kiss me, I grabbed her hips and flipped her over, pulling her over the edge of the table. I stood her in front of me and bent her over, shoving her chest down to the table. I yanked her jeans down as far as they would go, bunching them up against her boots. Then I knelt down and finished what I'd started, eating her upside-down. Just Katie's pussy and my face...

No more interruptions.

Fuck.

That sweet, slightly musky, heady taste of her... Katie's sex. I was totally fucking addicted to it. I ate her out with a passion, with a vengeance, with a fucking fury. I worked her clit with my tongue, sucked on her, until I shoved her right over the edge.

"Say it," I told her as she came, still eating her out. "Tell me you love me."

"Ah… Jesse… I totally love you…"

"Fuck, yeah," I mumbled, fucking her with my tongue as she shivered and shook.

When there was nothing left of her but a gasping puddle on the table, I stood up and turned her toward me, pulling her into my arms as she collapsed against me. Then I kissed her, good and hard.

"Come on." I scooped her up and threw her over my shoulder one last time, making her squeal.

"Aren't we gonna fuck?" she complained, sounding dazed and confused as I carried her up the stairs to the loft—the master bedroom.

"Not yet," I said.

"Oh, God… that was so unsatisfying."

I laughed as I threw her down on the king size bed.

I kicked off my boots and tore off my socks. I unbuckled my belt and unzipped my jeans, peeling them down, letting my cock free, heavy and thick with need. Letting her look at it. Her eyes darkened and she swiped her lip with her little pink tongue.

"Don't worry. I've got something to satisfy you…"

I stripped off my jeans, and Katie took off her jacket and sweater. I barely had my shirt over my head before I was on her, naked. Working myself between her legs. Her jeans and boots stayed on. She still had a tank top on, but I yanked that shit up. I shoved her bra up with it, letting her tits bounce loose.

"Ow!" she said. "Underwire…"

"Deal with it."

Then I was all over her, my face buried in her tits, my hand between her legs, my finger on her clit.

She smacked my ass, but groaned as I caressed her. Smooth and fast… just to make sure she was still with me. Her pussy was slippery-wet—from her arousal, her orgasm, from my spit. I sucked a nipple into my mouth and spread her thighs wide. Then I drove into her, my cock like a heatseeking missile, pre-programmed to hit home. I didn't have to think. I just had to fuck. Had to fuck *her*, in those furry boots that were digging into my ass.

Just smother myself in Katie.

It wasn't romantic.

It was frantic.

It was hungry and it was messy and it was fast. I bit her lip. She pinched my balls with her fingernails as we grappled and groped.

It sort of hurt.

She ended up half on top, hogtied around me by her jeans, then on the bottom again. I fucked her harder than I'd ever tried to fuck her. Once, I whispered, "This okay?" before she nodded and I kept at her. But I never really stopped.

Yes, she whispered, once.

Twice.

Yesss…

She made sounds I'd never heard her make. Sawed-off syllables supposed to be words, rasps and half-realized gasps, torn apart with need. Her voice shredded in the half-dark.

"Jesse, don't stop," she begged as I pounded her, when she knew I was close. She knew all the signs. She could hear it in my breath. Feel it in my cock, like a steel post, rigid inside her. Swollen… my balls pulled up tight. An itchy trigger just aching for release as I thrust into her. But I had control. I could hold back.

I didn't want to.

I was totally fucking sex-drunk.

I was Katie-drunk.

And I wanted to drown myself in it.

"Not gonna stop," I managed to say. "Until I blow. You gonna beat me there…?"

My question hung between us like a taunt. Like a tease.

She was already close. Her body was tightening around me, bearing down, coiling tight… sucking me in… "You're amazing," she whispered, her eyelids fluttering as I kissed her, and then she sighed. I thrust up into her. I ground my pelvis against her.

Her breath caught.

Then she came.

I rode her, hard, tumbling into it with her, both of us falling apart.

Her fingernails were pressed a half inch into my flesh.

Her furry boot was up my ass.

And I laughed a little.

Because that's what you did when you were drunk with ecstasy and the woman of your dreams had you in her arms, wrapped up in her damp thighs… lost inside her body. When she drank you in.

I collapsed there in her arms, heaving, just trying to catch my breath, and laughed.

"What's funny?" she panted after a while.

"Nothing's funny," I said with a sigh. "That's why I'm laughing."

Chapter Three

Katie

I stared at my husband's muscular ass as he bent over, digging around for something in the pocket of his jeans, which he'd discarded on the floor by the bed.

Husband.

Wow… that had an amazing ring to it.

Jesse Mayes was my husband.

My husband was Jesse Mayes… brown-eyed, badass rock star… and the most beautiful man I'd ever met, inside and out.

Just… *wow.*

He caught me staring at his ass and grinned, all cocky and sexy.

Then he yanked off my remaining clothes and flopped onto the bed next to me.

We both rolled onto our stomachs, lying naked and side-by-side, so close together his warmth radiated into me. The hairs on his thigh tickled me. Itched a little, actually, since I was all sweaty. But I was deliciously spent, my pulse still thrumming, and I couldn't be bothered to shift away.

So I sighed and relaxed, my face smushed into my pillow. It smelled of fresh northern air and cedar luxury cabin and Jesse.

He was propped up on his elbows, and I watched as he unfolded a little piece of note paper.

"What's that?"

"A little wedding night gift." His molten-dark eyes met mine. "I wrote some vows for you."

I smiled like a fool in love, unable to help myself. "We already did that part. Remember? All that 'I will always love you and honor you' stuff?"

"Yeah, but this is the really important stuff. Private vows. Too important to share in front of all those fucking voyeurs."

I giggled. "Such as?"

"Such as…" His brown eyes burned into me, all earnest passion. "I will always put you first. No matter what's going on with the band or anything else, if you need me, I'm here."

I leaned up and kissed him. "I know that, Jesse."

I did.

Jesse had been with Dirty since they were little more than kids. Ten years. And he'd known some of the band and crew even longer than that. They were his friends *and* his family.

But I was now his wife, and I knew what that meant to him.

"I needed to say it anyway," he murmured against my lips.

"I understand. And I'm okay with sharing you," I told him. "With Jessa. I mean… I know you're all she's got."

I knew that Jesse's sister, while so beautiful and successful and seemingly together on the outside, was alone. It was aching off her, that loneliness. I'd never been so sure of it as when she showed up at our wedding, looking so happy for us—and so totally unsure of where she fit in.

"If she needs you," I said, "I would never begrudge her that."

I meant it. I had an entire family to turn to if I needed support; Jessa didn't. She had Jesse, and she'd had him long before I came along. I'd promised myself when I agreed to marry him that I would never get in the way of that relationship. How could I? It was a bond that had been forged when Jessa was born and Jesse was only four; when he'd named her, after himself.

"Jesus, I love you," he said. Then he kissed me again. It was slow and hot, and I opened for him, taking him deep.

When he pulled away, his pupils were dilated. He licked his lip and groaned a little. I grinned.

Then he turned back to his little paper.

"Now quit distracting me. I have more vows to get through."

I brushed a little curl of his dark hair back from his face as he spoke, then trailed my fingertips over his shoulder and down his back, scraping him lightly with my nails, making him shiver. I had no intention of quitting; distracting Jesse was one of my favorite pastimes.

"I will always make sure you have a place to do your art. Or whatever it is you want to do."

"That's really sweet," I said. And it was. Especially when he'd already given me an amazing art studio where I could paint, and also let me set up a second, smaller studio in the sunroom of his house. *Our* house.

"I will always listen to your problems," he said, "and hold back your hair when you barf, and be patient with your moods." He glanced at me sidelong. "Even when you're on the rag and you get weepy."

"Amazing," I said, with somewhat-mock adoration. "So gallant, babe."

"Thank you. I try."

"So that means you'll eat ice cream with me and listen to me bitch about my cramps? And not judge me when I cry at cute puppy food commercials?"

I saw the gears turning in his head as he thought his way out of that one.

"I will always call someone in to do the stuff I don't wanna do, so it gets done," he said carefully.

I tried to peek at his paper, but he held it out of reach. "That's not even on there!"

"So? I mean it, babe. You've got PMS, I'll call Devi over in a heartbeat."

"Okay. That's fair." My best friend would be far more empathetic in such circumstances anyway.

"I promise to make you come almost every day—"

"Almost!?" I tickled that sensitive little notch at the base of his spine, making him buck a little. Goosebumps rippled across his flesh.

His eyes darkened as he gazed down at me. "Can't have you getting too used to that shit and taking it for granted. You'll get lazy."

"That's so flattering, sweetie," I said brightly.

"Besides…" He leaned in and kissed my temple, his lips lingering. "We both know you usually come more than once when we have sex. So in the long run, you're at a surplus."

"I like the math on that."

He kissed his way down my cheek toward my mouth. "I promise to keep you stocked with a lifetime supply of thongs… those lacy ones made of expensive dental floss…"

"Ugh." He slipped his tongue in my mouth, and for a long moment I got lost in his kiss. When he pulled away and grinned, leaving me a little breathless, I accused, "That vow's for you, though, not for me. Those things are gross. They ride up my butt."

"Yeah, but you've got a killer butt." He scanned his paper, maybe looking for something to make up for that one. "I promise to hire a personal trainer for you if you start to get fat?"

I pinched his butt cheek. Hard. "Lame! And grounds for divorce." He grinned a wicked grin, making me wonder if that one was even on the paper. "Unless it's my idea. Otherwise, I'll get as fat as I damned well want to."

He lowered his eyelids and gave me the same blatant eye-fucking he'd given me the first time we met… and countless times since. "I promise to do you, even if you get fat."

"Well, thank you. I guess."

"That one wasn't even written down. I improvised."

I squeezed his ass and gave him an overly-sweet smile. "And I promise to do *you*, even if you get fat *and* bald."

"Aww. Don't make me cry." He looked a little misty-eyed, and as usual, I couldn't even tell if he was faking or not. The man was a born performer. "I promise to clean up Max's shit even though I don't want to."

I smiled at that; a genuine smile. "Well, me and Max thank you." One thing Jesse knew: a direct route to my heart was definitely through my dog. I traced little circles, idly, on his butt. "You know," I mused, "if he didn't approve of you, I probably wouldn't have married you…"

He cocked a skeptical eyebrow. "I promise to try anything you want in bed at least once."

"Anything…?" My fingers crept toward his butt crack.

"Anything." He swatted my hand away. "Don't abuse it. Oh, this one's key. I promise if you get bored of me," he said importantly, "I'll make myself more interesting."

I laughed, hard. "That's… shit. I don't even know what to say to that. Thanks?"

"You're welcome."

My hand had found its way back to his ass, and my fingertip crept between his butt cheeks again. I just loved making him squirm…

"I promise I won't fart in bed unless I really, really have to," he said, straight-faced.

I snatched my hand back. "Ew."

"What? That's how much I respect you." He leaned in and gave me a quick, soft kiss I didn't return.

"Okay... So you'll still respect me if I have to?"

"Not allowed."

"What?"

"Deal-breaker."

I laughed, pushing him away. "What am I supposed to do? What if I'm sick or something?"

"Crawl into the bathroom and shut the door behind you."

"You are such a pig."

He kissed me again, his lips lingering suggestively on mine as his tongue teased the sensitive inner flesh of my upper lip. "You married me."

I fought the urge to open my mouth to his kiss... and suck his tongue right out of his head, the way he liked. "Are you done yet?"

"You don't like your special vows?" He nipped at my bottom lip with his teeth and tingles spread through my stomach, into my core. I was getting wet. Warming... softening to him.

Wanting him again.

"I love them." I rearranged myself on my side so I could wrap my arms around his neck and nuzzle his ear. "But there are a lot of them, sweetie. And I wanna be able to remember them all—in case you break any." I licked his earlobe and sucked it into my mouth, scraping lightly with my teeth because I knew it drove him crazy.

"Alright." He cleared his throat, rustling his little paper. "There's... uh... a bunch more sex stuff on here." His eyes locked on mine. "Or should I just skip it, and show you instead?"

I bit my lip.

He crumpled the paper and tossed it aside.

———

He kissed me, deep, his body melding to mine until we were pressed together, my nipples hard and tingling against his chest, his cock hard and pulsing against my stomach, my pussy throbbing with reawakening desire…

He kissed his way down my neck and I closed my eyes. Some of the urgency, the edge that had accompanied that first post-wedding fuck had been released, and now I could just bask in his touch… slow, exploratory, deliciously patient… yet hungry, as Jesse's touch always was.

He continued downward, closing his warm lips around one nipple, biting lightly, then flicking with his tongue. I gasped and arched into him, wanting more, but he released the nipple, just teasing, leaving feather-soft kisses on my skin.

"I promise not to leave you," he murmured against my other breast as he kissed the soft swell of flesh. His eyes lifted to mine beneath his dark, heavy lashes. "Unless you want me to."

"Never gonna happen," I breathed as he teased that nipple into his mouth and sucked. "Unless… you eventually get tired of me… and want to replace me with a newer model."

"Never gonna happen. And by the way, even if you wanted me to leave you," he added, kissing his way down my belly, "I'd probably stick around a while. You know, until it got really pathetic—"

"Uh-uh." I caught his face in my hands and tipped his head up. "I love you, Jesse Mayes," I whispered, holding his gaze.

His brown eyes softened as he looked up at me. "I love you, too…" he murmured against my skin, "… Mrs. Mayes."

I frowned. "I told you not to call me that. That's an old lady name."

"You are my old lady," he mumbled, kissing his way in a circle around my navel.

I stirred, growing restless and needy at his slow, teasing touch. "Jesse… don't start that crap…"

He dipped into my navel with his tongue, making me squirm. He knew that spot was hardwired to my clit; plus, it tickled. Then he fluttered his tongue down my naked belly, straight toward my—

"Oh, shit!" I sat up, shoving him off, and wriggled out from beneath him.

"The hell are you going?" He grabbed at me but I squirmed away, rolling out of bed.

"I have a wedding night gift for you, too!" I dashed into the en suite bathroom; I couldn't believe I'd almost forgotten.

"If you have to fart," he called after me, "just say so."

I rolled my eyes at him and slammed the door.

Chapter Four

Jesse

I lay sprawled across the bed, naked, waiting for Katie. Looking at myself in the mirrored ceiling.

What was it about looking at yourself, naked and spread out on a bed, from above, that was so... erotic? Not in a cocky way, but there was just something... Something about that view.

Yourself, submissive.

Maybe it was getting a glimpse of yourself the way your lover must see you. When she had you laid out, at her mercy...

My dick twitched at that thought, and I frowned at it, lying there half-soft.

"Babe, hurry up," I called out, as I gave my cock a few pumps. "I'm gonna fall asleep."

That wasn't true. I was too wired to sleep. I just wanted her to bring her sweet ass back out here so I could fuck her again before she got too distracted and lost the mood. One go with Katie was never enough. Especially after waiting for two fucking days.

Seconds later, the bathroom door swung open.

"Hey," she said, a smile in her slightly-husky voice, "quit touching yourself."

I rolled over to face her. "Why? You want all this hard di —*Whoa*."

Katie stood in the doorway to the bathroom, decked out in white lingerie; some kind of slutty-bride thing.

The fucking works.

A skimpy, see-through lace corset-thing with barely any material but just enough engineering to shove her boobs up—way up; garter straps clipped to sheer stockings; skimpy-as-fuck panties. And who could miss the *fuck-me-right-now* shoes… strappy high-heeled contraptions built for sex, because they sure as shit weren't built for comfort. They stacked about five extra inches onto her petite frame.

"Holy Christ."

I knelt up on the bed to stare at her.

Katie always wore sexy shit, but nothing like this. Tiny cotton panties, sexy as all hell on her, and a smooth pushup bra or no bra at all were more her thing. I'd never seen her in this much see-through, lacy stuff. And all that white against her creamy skin, her naturally rosy cheeks, her dark hair… totally fucking stunning.

I got up and met her halfway to the bed and gripped her waist, drawing her toward me. Then I kissed her. Her mouth, so hot and silky-wet, reminding me of her slippery-wet pussy, undid me. My cock was already aching for her again, stiff. I needed to fuck her, now. I could think of nothing else but whatever was the best position to screw her in all this sexy stuff.

Throw her down on her stomach?

On her back?

Bend her over…

My hands skimmed up her sides and I felt her shudder beneath the lace. She was breathing shallow and fast as we kissed;

her breasts heaved against me. The corset was fucking tight. A see-through vice.

She put her hands on my chest, her fingernails digging in as our kiss deepened. Then her hands slid down, down... and stroked my cock. One slow, teasing pump...

Then they were gone.

I felt her fumbling around below. She broke our kiss and looked down. She was struggling to unhook the straps clipped to her stockings.

"I want these stupid panties off!" she panted, frustrated. "Like right now. How are you supposed to fuck in all this stuff? It's like a chastity belt..."

I watched her struggle and swear, amused.

She managed to get one of the hooks loose from a stocking, ripping it in the process. "Oh, shit. I didn't know it would be so hard to take off..." She bit her lip a little, gazing up at me. "I wanted to do a little strippy thing for you."

I raised an eyebrow, liking that idea. "A strippy thing?"

"Yeah. Like a show. You know, peel it off, all sexy and suave." Her cheeks turned pink. "I've never done this before. I guess clothing that's actually easy to strip is kinda key."

"Uh-huh. That's why dudes wear those velcro pants." I kissed her again. "You're adorable, babe. But don't strip it off. I wanna fuck you in it."

"All of it?"

"Most of it." I slid my hand down between her legs, stroking her through the lace panties. "And for future reference... there's lingerie you wear to strip for a guy, and there's lingerie you wear to get fucked in. This is lingerie you get fucked in."

"Oh. Okay. It *was* kinda murder putting it on..."

"Katie," I told her, kissing her again and walking her toward the bed, "you don't have to wear this shit for me." Not that I didn't appreciate it... "You know that, right?"

"I just wanted it to be special," she murmured as she kissed my throat, her arms going around my neck. "I mean, we've already done everything there is to do…"

"Everything?"

She blushed as she gazed up at me. "Maybe not everything. Close."

"Okay." I stood her by the bed and got down on my knees. "I'm gonna show you what we can do…"

Then I kissed my way down her body. The parts covered in lace. The naked parts. I licked her along the edge of her panties. I nudged my nose against her clit, teasing her, then slipped a finger inside the lace and teased the crotch aside.

I swiped the tip of my tongue over her softness, making her shudder. I could eat Katie out all fucking night. Since she'd just married me, she was just gonna have to put up with my oral fixation.

Not like she didn't know about it from our very first date.

"You know I'm not gonna complain about *that*…" she said breathily, as she played with my hair. "But what's new? We have to do something new on our wedding night, Jesse."

Despite her half-hearted protests, I could feel the tension and the heat building between her legs. I groaned as I breathed her in. She was muskier now, her scent even headier, the way it always was after my cock had been between her legs.

"We did new stuff…"

She shifted, restless against me as I delved my tongue deeper. I sucked on her delicate lips and she gasped like she didn't mean to, rocking her hips into me.

"Like what?" she whispered.

"Like…" I teased her with my tongue between my words. "I ate you out on a staircase… That was new… I made you come under a deer antler chandelier… That was definitely new."

"That's just new decor," she breathed. "It doesn't count."

I looked up at her. Her face was flushed and her eyes were slightly hooded. They sparkled with lust as she gazed down at me.

I stood up, my chest brushing hers. I gripped her by the back of her neck and drew her close, brushing my lips against hers. "You're my wife. That's new. And it's more than enough to get me off."

It was true.

Katie Bloom—Katie *Mayes*—turned on... Was there any-fucking-thing sexier?

Nope.

My *wife*.

Damn...

I kissed her, deep, filling her mouth with my tongue like I owned it... sinking into the taste of her. I breathed her in... that familiar, sweet scent of vanilla, of cherries and cream.

That smell that always got me so fucking hard.

Katie Fucking Mayes.

I slid a hand down, into her panties. "Let me just help you with these." Then I thrust a finger right through the thin lace, ripping out the crotch.

"Oh," she gasped, glancing down. "*That's* how you do it without taking the rest off."

"Uh-huh..."

I lay her back on the bed, crawling right over her, and wrapped her silky, stocking-covered legs around me. Her stiletto heel bit into my ass and I growled.

"Oh! I can take off the shoes, if—"

"Fuck, no. Keep the shoes. Fucking love you in shoes..." I got busy kissing her neck, licking and sucking, lost in the smell of her. "Katie... whatever it is you do to smell so fucking good... don't ever change it."

"Jesse," she breathed, her hands roaming down my back. "Your butt looks... Wow. You have a nice ass." She squeezed my ass with both hands as she checked me out in the mirrored ceiling.

I kissed my way down, between her tits, which were still shoved up by her corset, against the forces of gravity. "Quit objectifying me…" I mumbled, my voice muffled by her cleavage. Katie had epic tits. Not huge, but full and perky on her petite, curvy frame. I once told her they were fat, as a compliment, but she didn't like that. Go figure.

She arched into my kisses. "Since when do you have a problem with being objectified?"

"Since it's distracting you from this." I swiped my tongue inside the cup of the corset and sucked her nipple out. I teased the hard pink tip with my teeth until she was gasping, squirming with need beneath me. Katie never could stay still when I touched her tits; I could *almost* make her come just by sucking on them.

I was pretty bent on getting her there one day.

"I just thought of one more vow," I told her. "And you're gonna like this one."

"Yeah?" she breathed.

"Yeah." I sucked her nipple into my mouth and teased the hell out of it with my tongue, then released it with a pop.

"*Ungghh…*" she groaned, which was Katie's incoherent way of saying, *Do that again.*

I switched to her other nipple, popping it out of the corset and teasing with flicks of my tongue, interspersed with soft, feathery kisses.

"I promise," I told her as she panted beneath me, "to keep finding new ways to fuck you. So it always feels like our wedding night."

She giggled, but it came out as a breathy sigh. "You're a true romantic, Jesse."

"You doubt my creativity, babe?"

"Well, no. I just—"

Then I spread her thighs, and sank my dick into her.

I watched her bite her lip to keep from crying out as I started stroking, in and out, but not too deep...

"I mean, really..." she said, her voice all soft and raspy. "How many different ways are there to fuck a girl?"

I tossed her a loaded look before returning my attention to her tits.

"If it's you, babe?" I let my stubbly chin rasp against her breast—she wouldn't let me go clean-shaven, even for our wedding. Said she loved me with a few days' growth. I was pretty sure she just loved the feel of it between her legs. "Fuck... endless possibilities..."

"That may be the dirtiest thing you've ever said to me, Jesse," she said sweetly.

"Just feels that way because my dick is inside you..."

"Mmm." She squirmed, raising her hips to take me deeper, urging me to it, and as I sank home, she gasped, "You're right." She rocked her hips against me. "But you say a lot of things dirtier than other people do..."

"It's a gift. Stop squirming."

Then I held her down, pinning her hips as I drove into her, making her take me the way I wanted her to—at my pace. I controlled the rhythm, the depth. And as I watched her take my cock, her tits heaved, spilling from her corset. She probably couldn't get a full breath in that thing.

"Is it wrong that you're kinda suffocating and it's turning me on?"

"No," she breathed. "It's kinky."

"Good. Then I'm gonna say... that's new. I've never seen you actually struggle to breathe while I fucked you before."

"I always struggle to breathe while you fuck me."

"Flattery," I mumbled, leaning down to run my tongue

between her breasts again… and over the swollen curves, the hard tips.

"Truth," she whispered, arching her back for more. "Did you mean it, though? The 'always' part?"

"Hmm?"

"You're always gonna think of new ways to fuck me?"

"Mmm," I mumbled against her sweet skin as the blood left my head. She was covered in the lightest sheen of sweat. I could feel her pussy burning up, swelling, tightening around me, choking me as she fought to move her hips against mine. "When I'm not too tired," I said, fucking her slow… lapping her nipples with my tongue. "And, you know, if I'm not mad at you."

"What…? What… um… happens if you're mad at me?"

I paused, meeting her sex-hazed eyes, then fucked her harder for effect. Once. Then again. Hard… but slow.

"Then I'll just spank your ass and fuck the hell out of you, and you'll like what you get."

She bit her full bottom lip, twisting it in her teeth as I sped up my thrusts. "Oh, God. Shit. It's really unfair how much that just turned me on…"

I smiled and kissed her.

Then an idea occurred to me, and I stilled. Katie undulated beneath me like a snake—a snake bound in lace, breathless, sucking hungrily at my tongue.

"Baby…" she begged.

"Just a sec."

Then I tore myself from her grip and pulled my dick out, getting up. She started to sit up, awkwardly, impeded by her corset. "But—!"

"Hold that thought." I sprang out of bed and dashed into the bathroom. I didn't want to leave her hanging any more than she wanted to be left.

"Jesse?" she called after me, all breathy and confused. "Jesse

Mayes…? Did you seriously just *stop* in the middle of fucking me?"

––––––

I found Katie's makeup bag on the bathroom counter and started rooting through it. Where the fuck were they? I knew she kept them in here…

I heard her sigh and flop back on the bed.

"Does trying new things involve some sort of cross-dressing thing?" she called. "Because if so, you really don't need mascara. Women pay a lot of money to get eyelashes like yours. Jesse…?"

"Uh-huh…"

"In other words, you'd make a gorgeous chick. If one could look past all the muscles and the body hair. But I can't say I want to."

"How do you know until you try?"

As I strode back into the bedroom, she propped herself up on her elbows and threw me a skeptical pout.

"We've never done *this* before," I said, holding up a packet of her birth control pills.

"You know that's birth control, right?" she said, teasing. "It's not, like, ecstasy. Or Viagra."

"Viagra? Woman, please." I popped the little pills into my hand one by one until the case was empty. Then I raised an eyebrow at Katie in silent question.

She looked at the pile of pills in the palm of my hand. Then she met my eyes.

She bit her lip a little… and nodded.

My heart thumped in my chest. Because *damn.*

I'd been planning to bring it up. Soon. Maybe not tonight.

But why the fuck not?

I slipped off one of her sexy shoes and crushed the pills to dust on the bedside table with the heel.

"Great," she said. "Now the staff will think we snorted lines off there or something."

"I'm a rock star, babe," I said. "They already think that."

"You know doing that isn't gonna make me insta-pregnant, right?"

"Don't be a smart-ass. It's symbolic."

I tossed her shoe aside and dove on top of her. My cock, still half-mast, pressed to the inside of her thigh as I kissed her, deep. She kissed me back, but I could feel her resistance. She'd tensed up. Way up.

"You're... um... really committed to this... doing-something-new thing," she said, giggling a little between kisses.

"Yup."

"You know," she mused, as I sucked my way down her throat, "a baby would be crazy new."

"Uh-huh."

"Might impede your ability to stick to your other vows, though..."

I looked at her, mildly offended. "Like what?"

"Making me come every day?"

I slipped my hand between her legs and slid my middle finger, slowly, up into her. So fucking smooth, hot and wet... I watched her eyes haze over and her mouth drop open as she relaxed a little.

"*Almost* every day," I said, my voice rough with lust. "And besides..." I told her, teasing one of her blushing nipples with my tongue, "I don't see why a baby would impede that."

She laughed softly, digging her hands into my hair as I kissed my way between her breasts. "That's because you've never had one, sweetie."

"Neither have you."

"Yet I know enough to know that orgasms may slide down the priority list for a while once I do."

"Then I'll just have to pull up that other vow... Call someone in to deal with shit for me."

Katie's hands stilled in my hair. "To give me orgasms?"

"The baby, wise-ass." I bit her nipple lightly and fucked her slowly with my finger. "I'll hire a nanny to help with the baby, so we still have time for orgasms."

"It's not just time, you know," she panted, as I worked her back up. "It's... energy. We'd be tired as shit, getting up all night with a newborn. And my boobs would be all full of milk... and sore... and you wouldn't get to oral-fetish on me all the time..."

I looked at her, lifting myself off her a bit as I withdrew my finger from her pussy. "Do I need to scrape those pills back together?"

She smiled, pulling me back on top of her. "No. Just saying. But we'll just have to deal with it like we do everything else." She wrapped her thighs around my hips. "Together," she said softly.

"Yeah," I agreed. "Together." I rubbed the length of my hard cock against her softness, all slick and warm and ready for me.

"Please, Jesse..." she purred as she kissed me.

"God, I love it when you beg..."

"Just give it to me, for fuck's sake," she said. "I didn't marry you so you could fuck off into the bathroom halfway to my next orgasm..."

I grinned. "You've always had a way with dirty words yourself, you know that?"

"Only with you," she murmured, shifting beneath me. She was trying like hell to line up the head of my cock with her wet pussy. Too bad for her, I outweighed her by a hundred bucks.

I grabbed her hands and pressed them into the bed, above her head. Then I used my full weight to pin her down, my cock lined up—but just out of reach.

Then I looked her in the eye and asked her, "Yeah?"

She smiled, even as she panted with anticipation. "It's not magic, and it's not instant, you know. I'm not gonna get pregnant tonight. It's not even the right time in my cycle—"

"Don't be a party pooper, Katie. I told you, it's symbolic."

At that, her eyes softened. She reached up to kiss me with her sweet, full lips… and that light touch, Katie's warm breath against my face, feeling her need building as she panted in her corset, so hungry I could almost taste it… it sent lighting bolts of lust ripping down my spine.

"Then, yeah," she whispered.

I rammed into her then, deep. She cried out as she took me, biting my lip. Then I thrust my tongue in her mouth, filling her at both ends as I drove into her, again and again.

She murmured against my lips when I eased up to let her breathe, begging me for more.

"Harder, Jesse… I wanna be yours…"

"You are mine."

Her tits swelled against me as my weight and the corset smothered her, and when she came, it was with a desperate, ragged, feral cry like nothing I'd ever pulled from her before.

God… Jesse…

Yes…

It pushed me right over the edge.

I shoved into her, coming like a rocket, just blanking out and giving in as I collapsed against her… Riding the waves of ecstasy as our bodies melded, shuddering together.

My fingers laced through hers, I squeezed her hands.

And afterward, when I could move again, just enough to see her face… to shift myself to the side so I didn't crush her… I looked into her big blue-green eyes. And she looked back at me.

"I promise," I told her in a rough whisper, "I'll be a good dad, Katie. Actually, I'm pretty sure… I'll be an exceptional dad."

She smiled, and happy tears sparked in her eyes. "I know you will, Jesse."

And in that moment, I saw it, so clear: a little girl or a boy with those eyes, and Katie's sweet smile…

And I fell in love with her all over again.

A Dirty Secret

Author's Note

If you've read *Dirty Like Us*—and you really, really should before reading this story, *A Dirty Secret*—then you know the big secret about Dirty's lead singer, Zane Traynor, and Maggie Omura, the band's assistant manager. There are a couple of scenes in *Dirty Like Brody* that address it as well. So if you want every last detail of Zane and Maggie's story so far, you'll need to read the other books first.

Dirty Like Brody takes place many months after Zane and Maggie's crazy night in Las Vegas in *Dirty Like Us*, and for all that time, they've both kept their secret.

But what's been going on behind the scenes? Are they fucking or what? More importantly, are they in love? Whatever's going on, why is it all still a secret? And what the hell are they going to do about it?

Well, as the pragmatic Maggie puts it in *Dirty Like Brody*, it's complicated. And to quote her: "If I knew the answers to such questions... I wouldn't be drinking wine straight from the bottle."

The night of Jesse and Katie's wedding in *Dirty Like Brody*, we see Maggie, in her wet undies, being hauled off into the woods, caveman style, by a naked Zane after their midnight swim.

So what the heck happens next?

I'll give you one guess…

Jaine

Chapter 1

Maggie

I sat back and watched as my good friend, Jessa, did something I never thought she'd do: she walked straight out the dock, stripped down to her underwear, and hopped into the just-slightly-above-freezing waters of Cathedral Cove.

I laughed and applauded wildly.

Seconds later, her head popped above water. "Jesus!" she screamed. "Fuck, that's cold!" And I kept laughing—from my cozy, dry seat by the fire.

It was January and this was Canada; we were way up on the Pacific Coast of Vancouver Island, but with the fire—and several layers of clothing—it was fine. The naked crazies in the water could suit themselves. I was more than happy where I was.

It was the middle of the night and we'd been drinking and singing songs, jamming around the fire pit—just the members of Dirty, the mega-successful rock band I'd co-managed for almost seven years, and a few close friends. It was the night of our lead guitarist's wedding; Jesse Mayes—Jessa's brother—had just married his fiancee, Katie Bloom. The wedding was incredible and the party had gone late, but only a few of us had lasted this long.

Jesse and Katie had disappeared up to their lux newlyweds' cabin a while ago, and while I was privately jealous that they were most definitely fucking like bunnies right now... as a girl who hadn't gotten any in a lot longer than I liked to think about—well, I was trying not to think about it.

Likely, some of us were still up because we were still hoping to hook up, while the rest of us just weren't ready for the party to end, for reasons of our own.

I was looking right at my reason.

Zane Traynor, lead singer of Dirty; the living definition of a rock god. The man with the biggest ego of any man I'd ever met, but the killer voice, gorgeous face and otherworldly body—big, swinging dick and all—to back it up. No surprise, he was one of the crazies in the water. Actually, he'd kinda led the naked charge.

I watched as he threw his arms around Jessa, his slicked-back blond hair gleaming in the moonlight. I couldn't see them clearly in the near-dark, just their heads bobbing on the water, but some-how, I knew Zane was watching me.

"Maggie!" he hollered as he held Jessa close. "Get your ass in the water!" For a split second I let myself wonder if he'd ever fucked her; I wondered that about most women who got near Zane.

At least, the hot ones.

But no, I concluded as I sipped my beer. Zane and Jessa had never fucked, even though she was super-hot. Mainly because she would never do that to me.

Thank Christ, for both her sake and mine.

"Don't let the old man cramp your style, Maggs," Ash put in. The lead singer for the alt rock band Penny Pushers, Ash was also in the water, along with our drummer, Dylan, and Roni, a girlfriend of Jessa's; the lot of them were all amped up on liquid courage. All except Zane, who didn't drink.

Unlike regular mortals, Zane didn't need booze to fuel his crazy.

I glanced over at my boss, Brody, Dirty's longtime manager and close friend, who was sitting beside me, and rolled my eyes. Old man, was it?

When even Dylan started mouthing off at us next, I knew it was dawning on all of them what total morons they were, freezing their asses off while Brody and I lounged by the fire pit.

"Maggie May!" Zane thundered at me, using the full force of his lead singer's pipes and drowning everyone else out. "Get your ass in the water before my dick falls off!"

"Jesus Christ," I grumbled, but finally, I stood up. Because apparently there was a little moron inside me, too. "Doesn't he ever shut up?" I sucked back my beer and set it aside.

Brody didn't bother answering, just smirked and drank his beer.

I walked straight out the dock and did the only thing I knew for sure would shut Zane up. I stripped down to my underwear—quickly—to a bunch of appreciative catcalls, and jumped in the water.

And *fuck me*, it hurt.

Kinda like my body was crashing through ice.

I fought back to the surface as the pressure, at once numbing and so incredibly *burning*, squeezed in. I gasped brokenly for air. Then I screamed—the most bloodcurdling, jagged scream I'd ever heard, and until now, I didn't even know I could make.

My friends howled in the water around me.

I heard Jessa's teeth chattering as she said, "M-maggie, we're g-gonna d-d-die!"

Yep. Totally fucking felt that way.

Ash was already climbing out, the big man-baby, and

streaking buck-naked up the dock toward the trees; with all the tattoos and piercings, you'd think the guy could handle a little pain. Roni was next, then Dylan, also bare-assed. They dashed up the boardwalk and into the old-growth forest, leaving their clothes behind.

I was already doing a frantic doggy-paddle back to the dock myself—I'd never been the world's strongest swimmer—when Jessa, all long-limbed and lithe, glided past me and hauled herself up the ladder, water sheeting off her swimsuit model's body.

I was close behind, shaking so hard I thought my clawed hands might slip off the metal rail, but I made it up to the dock, wheezing. I'd never felt anything so shockingly fucking cold. And now the pain was *really* sinking in.

Yeah; fuck clothes.

I ran up the dock as fast as I dared, afraid of slipping in the near-dark, hugging myself so hard I thought my ribs might crack. Brody was on the dock with Jessa, wrapping her in a blanket, but I didn't see another blanket anywhere and I didn't stop.

I heard Zane behind me, roaring as he barreled up the dock. "Holy mother of fuck! My balls are up behind my eyeballs…" He grabbed me by the waist, swung me around, and threw me over his shoulder—like a fucking Neanderthal.

A scream tore from my lungs, partly out of relief. I should've told him to put me the fuck down, like now, but Jesus *fucking* Christ.

Never so cold in my life.

Instead, as he hauled me up the boardwalk, I slapped his bare ass as hard as I could. My hand on his wet cheek made a satisfying smacking sound; I would've hoped it hurt, but he was probably in too much pain to notice. "Do not drop me," I said. "I'm freezing!" Then the deeper dark of the woods swallowed us… and I got hit with a sickening rush of vertigo. "Oh my God, stop!"

Zane slowed down, but he didn't stop. "S'okay, Maggs," he

said, teeth chattering. Was that a sign of hypothermia? "I'll take you to your cabin."

"Just s-slow down," I ordered, my own teeth starting to chatter, and he slowed a little more. "It's so dark… I can't see shit except your ass and your f-feet flickering out of the dark. It's gross."

"Just shut up and tell me where your cabin is."

"I have a r-room," I said, "in one of the b-big ones, east of the lodge."

"Where the fuck is east?"

I tried to lift my head, looking around, but I couldn't see. Everything was passing in disorienting flashes. Snatches of trees and the boardwalk handrail catching the moonlight; pools of light pouring from the windows of cabins or the little yellow lights above the doors. Darkness; moonlight; yellow light; darkness.

And music. It had to be almost four in the morning, but we weren't the only ones still up.

"Jude," Zane remarked as we passed the cabin where the Stone Temple Pilots' "Sex Type Thing" was throbbing into the night. "Guy never sleeps. Probably got all the single chicks herded up in there…"

I didn't touch that. But clearly "all the single chicks" didn't include me.

It really should have.

Except that I wasn't single, not technically—and Zane was the only one who knew it.

He was right about Jude, though. Of all the guys in and around the band these days, it was Jude, our head of security, who was most likely to trash a hotel room—or in this case, a luxury resort cabin. It didn't bother me, much, as long as he forked over a generous sum to cover the damages in the morning, along with a hefty tip.

"Whatever," I said. "Just g-get me to my cabin so I can p-put some pants on before anyone else s-sees me."

Because despite what I'd just done, I really didn't need a bunch of my coworkers seeing me in my wet underwear.

———

Somehow, I managed to guide Zane to my door, though we got lost in the labyrinth of the trees several times and had to backtrack.

He carried me inside, and I stumbled a bit as he put me down, kinda dizzy from the ride as I found my feet.

I wasn't drunk; I'd made that mistake with Zane once, and ended up with a hangover in the form of his naked body in my bed, a round of electrifying morning sex, and an engagement ring with a rock the size of Gibraltar. But this had been a long day—especially for me, since I'd helped organize the wedding—and I was wobbly with exhaustion and the painful ache of the cold in my bones.

Zane caught me, steadying me with his hands on my hips.

On reflex, my hands clamped onto his arms. We were both shivering as we stood there, frozen, locked together.

And then, predictably, he moved in.

We were alone, he was naked, I was near-naked; it really didn't take much. And he was definitely gonna kiss me.

Couldn't fault a guy for trying, right?

Wrong.

I dodged and dashed, extracting myself from his grip, and put space between us.

"You can go now," I said, hugging myself and hopping up and down. I held his gaze, carefully avoiding his cock. Because yes, he was *completely* naked. And I really didn't need to see *that.*

Even if I kinda really wanted to…

"Christ, Maggs, just let me warm up." He rubbed his hands up and down his arms and barreled past me, shivering.

"I'm too cold to fight with you, Zane," I snapped, still hopping around.

"Then don't."

"Don't you *dare* get into that bed all wet!"

I hurried into the bathroom as he headed toward my bed, emerging with a towel and throwing it at him. He got to work drying off, quickly, trying to warm himself as he rubbed the towel on his body. Not that I was watching…

Jesus, though. There were women who'd *pay* for this private show.

Shrinkage or no, the man was stunning. Lean, tall and blond, his sculpted body all tense and shivering from the cold, muscles twitching and flexing as he ran the towel over his long, hard thighs…

Video: Zane Traynor towels off after midnight skinny dip.
Instant viral sensation.

"You need to go, before I die," I gritted out between my teeth, still hopping as I turned away.

He ignored me, heading over to the fireplace. I tried not to peek as he bent down, his bare ass in the air as he rooted through the logs on offer, obviously intending to start a fire. Well, shit. I was hardly gonna stop him from that endeavor.

"Bloody *fuck*," I swore instead, giving up.

Then I dashed into the bathroom, slamming the door behind me, and blasted the shower on hot. Shaking, I dove right in, then gradually peeled off my wet panties and bra. I was so cold, it took several minutes before the warmth actually soaked in and my body started to register it. But when it did…

Pure ecstasy.

"You better quit making those sexy moaning noises…" Zane opened the glass shower door and stepped right into the spray, crowding into me. "If you expect me to keep my hands to myself."

I turned my back on him, fast. "Zane! Get the fuck out!"

"What? I'm warming up. You want *me* to die?"

I rolled my eyes and tried to ignore him. Which was totally fucking impossible. I edged forward as far as I could go and still get some of the spray, but he was right behind me. The bulk of his body—his pecs, his thighs, his fucking dick—brushing against me.

At least he wasn't hard. Yet.

"Quit hogging the water, Maggs," he said, pushing in closer behind me, and I stiffened as more of his body came into contact with mine... just lightly, nudging against me. He shivered violently—setting off a wave of goosebumps on my newly-warmed skin. Then he groaned, long and low, as the heat soaked into him. "*Jesus... fuck*, that's good..."

Fucking *hell*.

It was like listening to a live porno, custom-calibrated to my exact fantasies, only inches behind me.

Worse, his words reminded me of the things he'd said to me, and the *way* he'd said them to me, that first night we'd spent together.

Our wedding night.

"Get warm and get out, Zane," I said, my tone cool and detached. It was a well-practiced tone, used over many years in Zane Traynor's presence. The one that said, *I'm not buying your shit*, when I totally was.

Because this was the only defense I knew: denial.

My body was anything *but* cool as the hot water and Zane's increasing body heat began to smother me. My brain was no help either. My thoughts raced ahead, full-steam, imagining all the things my body could be doing with his, right now. I berated myself, half-heartedly, for failing to lock the bathroom door. But the truth was, I left it unlocked on purpose. Because apparently that little moron inside me just loved tempting fate.

So maybe there was no point in even trying to deny it anymore. It was beyond official: I was a masochist, plain and simple.

When it came to Zane, maybe I'd always been one.

Maybe I'd always *be* one.

He sighed raggedly, a sound of deep contentment. And I couldn't even pretend that I didn't like hearing him happy.

Because again, masochist.

"Babe," he said, his voice relaxed and husky in my ear, his breath and his devilish blond beard tickling my neck, "you think turning your back on me is making you any less of a temptation, you're stupider than I thought."

"What!?" I turned my head to skewer him with my eyes.

He gave me the world's most charming—yet evil—grin. Because he was messing with me. And I was falling for it.

And Zane just *loved* that shit.

"Whatever," I grumbled.

Damn, though. What the fuck was wrong with me?

I went to one wedding with Zane—well, besides our own—and I turned to useless, horny goo inside?

I'd promised myself, like pinkie-swear promised, after the last time I let him stick his giant dick inside me and fuck me into the stratosphere that it was the *last* fucking time. That from that day on, he would be nothing to me but a work associate. A sexless, boring-as-fuck colleague, afflicted with some nasty, putrescent venereal disease.

Yes, I'd totally made up the VD part—to trick myself into believing that Zane Traynor was *way* less appealing than he actually was. I'd even convinced myself—as I came down, sweating and shuddering, from that last Earth-shattering, mind-blowing orgasm—that tricking myself might just work.

Because I was desperate enough to believe it.

I would've believed anything, if I thought it might save me from getting naked with him again.

And now, here I was.

Naked.

With him.

Again.

"Take your 'temptation' and go, Zane," I said. "I just wanna be alone."

"No, you don't," he said, his tongue just happening to lick my neck as he spoke, slowly and lazily, almost like it was an accident. Which maybe it was. Hard be it for Zane to keep his dick in his pants or his tongue in his mouth when wet, naked pussy was to be had.

"Yes," I said firmly, "I do."

"Okay, how about this…" He edged in closer. His cock, which was now definitely hard, pressed against my butt. "We get warm *together*, then I go. *If* you still want me to." He said it like he didn't believe for a fucking second that if I let him get me warm, I'd want him to leave.

He was probably right about that.

And I fucking hated it that he was right.

"Just keep that thing away from me," I grumbled, as the familiar tension built, hot in my core, desire for him surging with an urgency that always threw me off-center.

Overwhelming.

Irresistible…

"What thing?" he prompted, not even feigning innocence.

I tossed him a dark glare over my shoulder and his wicked pierced eyebrow arched. Water droplets shimmered on his chiseled, godlike face and his dark eyelashes, spiky and wet, made his already-gorgeous ice-blue eyes even more striking. Totally reminded me of how he looked onstage toward the end of a show

—his clothes soaked through, his golden skin dripping with sweat…

So completely unfair that he looked even hotter soaking wet.

I probably looked like a drowned rat. Or a drowned raccoon; I hadn't even taken off my makeup.

"Your dick, asshole. Put it back in your pants."

"Why?" he asked, his dick still pressed against me as he smoothed his hands lazily through his wet hair.

"Because it's fucking dangerous."

"Dangerous?" I turned away but I could still hear the smile in his smug voice. "Just think of it as a loaded gun, babe. Only dangerous if you pull the trigger. And, sweetheart… your hands are on your tits."

I dropped my hands. *Damn…* He made it sound dirty, like I was groping myself, when all I was doing was trying to shield myself from him.

I couldn't exactly help it if my nipples had started throbbing as his dick pressed against me, my body going totally fucking haywire in response to his proximity… like it always did when Zane got me alone.

And I couldn't fucking take it.

Three months. That's how long it'd been since I got off with a man.

Three. Long. Months.

Since the last time I let Zane Traynor, my husband but not really my husband, fuck me to hell and back.

My latest lapse in sanity. Though probably not my last.

Because I had some sort of sickness. An inability to resist him for more than ninety days. A debilitating weakness for his smoking-hot voice, his cocky swagger, his blue eyes and his big dick.

Just to name a few.

Yeah; I glanced back at those blue eyes of his, and I knew it.

If I didn't get out of this shower, right now… I was fucked.

Chapter 2

Maggie

I sighed in frustration, and pressed my hands to the shower wall so I wouldn't touch anything else—Zane's or mine. And the worst part? He wasn't even touching me anymore.

He'd edged back a couple of inches so his dick was no longer feeling me up. It was fully erect, though, pointing at me like an accusation when I glanced back. Heavy, swollen, long, and totally unapologetic. There was nothing at all polite about that dick.

He knew it, and he didn't bother covering it up.

Fuck, but I wanted him inside me.

"Look…" I said, with some struggle. "You know exactly what you can do with that thing. What you do to women. I'm not gonna sit here on some high horse and pretend I'm immune, but—"

"Women?" he said, feigning confusion. "Like Jessa?"

I frowned. "No, not like Jessa, but—"

"Elle?"

Right. As Dirty's bass player and Zane's longtime bandmate, Elle probably wouldn't fuck Zane in a last-man-on-Earth scenario. They'd been friends too long, business partners too long, irritated the shit out of each other too long. "Well, no. Not Elle. Just—"

"Katie?"

I scowled. Jesse's new wife was so off limits to Zane it wasn't funny. And he knew it, too. Jesse would murder him in his sleep if he ever made any kind of serious play for her. "Not Katie. Don't even fucking say that."

"Hey, I'm just trying to follow, Maggs. You said I do something to women. I'm dangerous. Or my dick is. But I just named three women in like a split second who don't give a shit about my dick."

Jesus, the guy was irritating. "Okay, so maybe not *all* women—"

"So just you, then."

"Right. Just me," I said in my most sarcastic tone. "Go ahead and play innocent. Put this all on me. I don't care. Just get your big dick and your six pack and your blue eyes and your devil's smile the hell out of my shower, and go find someone else to harass."

"Harass?" He laughed his cocky laugh. "I'm just showering, babe. Getting warm. You're the one fixating on my dick."

"It's *hard*, Zane."

"It's a biological function," he said, eyelids lowering. He was so totally enjoying the fuck out of this. "I can't always control it."

"*I know*," I said, slowly and with all the ice I could summon in all this steaming heat. "That's kind of the fucking problem."

His smile faded, eyes narrowing. "What is?"

I turned to face him, covering my goods as well as I could with my hands. Not well enough. His gaze fell, molesting every inch of exposed skin.

"You and your dick," I said flatly, doing my best to ignore the throbbing between my legs, the way my breasts felt heavy, my nipples fucking ached, and my breathing was getting all rough and uneven. Because I *did* know exactly what he could do to me, in seconds, if I let him, and I was already wavering on that precipice between control and total abandon—between caring and totally not caring if fucking the shit out of Zane, right here and now, was a good idea. "The both of you are catnip for horny pussy, and you fucking know it."

His eyes lifted to mine. He blinked, once. Then he laughed, his infamous Viking laugh, big, bold and all-conquering, right in my face.

And for just that split second, control won out.

"Yeah, I'm going."

I darted into the narrow space between his large frame and the glass shower door.

I didn't get far.

He grabbed me by my waist and spun me around, pressing my back up against the tile wall. It was easy. He was big, I was small.

Plus, I didn't actually want to go. My control was so quickly abandoned, it was surreal; my head spun as he pinned me there. But I didn't fight.

So maybe I just wanted to protest a little before I gave in?

Shit. Did that make me sick? Kinda *felt* sick.

But maybe not in a bad way...

His fingers dug into my hips and held me tight as he pressed in, and a shudder of nervous anticipation ran through me.

"Horny pussy...?"

He wasn't laughing anymore. His gaze moved slowly down my face, from my eyes to my parted lips, like he was reading me. And I felt totally exposed. He could probably *smell* my arousal. The man was a total bloodhound when it came to sex *and* my discomfort.

And when Zane and I had sex, discomfort was always a part of it—for me.

Worse, I'd come to learn that my discomfort turned him on. As did my increasingly feeble protests.

Maybe to him, this was all just a long, slow, sometimes painful game that he was gradually winning.

But I really couldn't help any of it. The protests. The struggle. The giving in.

I wanted him, like I'd never wanted anyone in my life.

And… I wanted not to want him.

I was breathing too hard, hanging on by a thin thread. I pressed my hands to the wall behind me, spreading my fingers and trying to dig in, like I could somehow leech onto the tile. But my hips stirred in his hands, restless, and I bit my lip, twisting it in my teeth, hard.

"You telling me you're horny, Maggs?" he asked slowly, his smoky voice dropping dangerous-low. His tongue snaked out to lick his lip.

I swallowed.

"Telling me you're horny's a bad, bad move, Maggie May," he pressed, his mouth so close to mine I could feel his breath on my face. I could almost *taste* him. "If you want me out of this shower…"

"Get over yourself," I managed. But my voice was all breathy and pathetic.

"Why don't you just let me take care of that for you…" he said, casually, like he was offering to scratch an itch. "You know I can take care of it…" His thumbs stroked the indents between my hip bones and my groin, slowly.

And I knew I was getting wet down below, in a way that had nothing to do with the shower. My whole body was thudding, aching, hungry for him.

So fucking ready.

So fucking tired of waiting.

So fucking scared of giving in.

"But I really… I don't…" *Shit.* I was breathing faster, heavier, as the words failed me. And words rarely failed me.

His gaze dropped to my chest, which was heaving.

"Sure, you do," he murmured.

And I did. I so *fucking* did.

He knew it, and the shitty truth, I'd wanted him to know it.

Every single thing I'd said to him tonight—actually, for the duration of this entire event—had told him *Nuh-uh…* Yet the hunger behind every word, every stolen glance, had told him *Yes.*

Actually, it had told him *Please.*

Fucking please.

Give it to me.

I want it.

Hard. Fast. Just give it…

And he knew he could give it, that I'd take it, that I wouldn't actually stop him if he tried. But he hadn't tried; at least, not hard and fast.

Instead, he was taking his time, drawing this out; savoring it.

My discomfort. My resistance. My inner struggle…

Touch me.

Don't touch me.

Please fucking touch me.

"You looked pretty tonight, Maggie," he whispered. Then he smiled a little, the corner of his mouth curling up in that impish, boyish way it did when he was being cute. Not coy cute and not fake cute, not kiss-her-ass-because-I-want-to-do-her cute. Just cute.

And it made me go all stupid and squishy inside.

"Don't," I said. "Don't do that."

Lethal. Zane being sweet to me; it was as dangerous as his hard dick waving at me in a hot shower.

Actually, it was worse.

"Do what?"

"Don't be nice," I said.

"Okay. Have it your way." He moved in, shoving up against me. "I've got more practice being an asshole anyway."

He grabbed my hands and pushed them up above my head, pinning me against the wall. I felt every inch of his long, hard cock pressed against my stomach... so slippery and wet. I felt him throb against me as his desire surged, as he leaned into me with his weight. His balls, full and heavy and firm, pressed against my clit. His nipple piercing dug into my chest.

And it was kind of a relief.

I exhaled, like I'd been holding my breath all fucking night.

Then he said, "But you did look pretty," his blue eyes on mine. "In that little black dress, with your hair all twirled up..."

"Just shut up, Zane."

"Kept imagining what you were wearing underneath it," he went on, his hands digging into my wrists as he moved his hips, grinding his slippery dick against me. "And how you'd look with it all bunched up around your waist... while I bent you over and fucked you 'til you screamed." Then he tipped his face down as if to kiss me.

But he didn't.

Instead, he took his sweet fucking time.

"Fucking love it when you scream..." he murmured.

Then he fit his mouth to mine.

And it fit so fucking good, like he was born to kiss me. Like I was born to be kissed by him.

He did it slowly, too, just to rub it in. To give me all the chance in the world to pull away, to shove him off, to say no, to slap his face.

I did none of those things.

I opened to the slide of his wet lips, all slippery and warm, and I moaned desperately as he slid his tongue inside my mouth, hot and aggressive but slow… lapping against mine in a torturous dance that made my entire body curl up into him.

Then he slid his mouth away just as slowly, making me groan.

"More?" he asked with a half-smile. But this time it was a happy smile, not a cocky smile, his blue eyes dancing.

Joy, not victory.

Worse.

"Yes, more," I said, half-desperate, half-angry as I struggled to lean into him. But he held me pinned to the wall as he kissed me again; as I kissed him back.

And I closed my eyes, so I didn't have to see that terrible joy on his face.

He shifted my wrists into just one hand and, keeping them pinned, ran his other hand down, between my legs. I gasped as he touched me, my body responding in that way only he could make it respond, stroking all my sweet spots with just the right pressure… teasing at first, letting me warm up to his touch, and gradually delving deeper… making me want just that little bit more.

"More…" I whispered when he kissed his way down my neck, his finger slipping inside me. I bit his shoulder and groaned as a second finger joined the first.

"*Fuck*… We need a condom," he muttered. "I need to be inside you…"

I sighed, shuddering as his fingers moved inside me. "I have some."

"You have some?"

I opened my eyes to find him looking at me. A grin played at his lips, but I could tell he was trying to keep a damper on it. And it made me hella surly; the grin and the damper.

"Yeah," I said, twisting away from his hand. "So?"

He released my wrists and I crossed my arms over my chest, but he slid his hand back between my legs, unfazed. "Maggie

May," he said, stroking me slowly, "were you planning on getting laid at Jesse and Katie's wedding?"

I bristled, trying not to let what he was doing down below affect me, but *shit*. I was not that good an actress. "No. Not planning. Just… being prepared."

"Prepared." He seemed to roll the word around in his mouth, as he rolled his fingertips over my clit. "Because… you knew… once you saw me walk up the aisle in my suit, you'd just have to have me?"

I pushed his hand away and looked away, over his shoulder, when I said, "Because I know I can't trust you."

And that was true.

Simply put, I didn't know if I'd *ever* be able to trust a man who was so like my dad. That absent, self-involved and reckless man who had, unfortunately, shaped me, who'd cast a shadow of neglect over my whole life, yet had never actually been *real* to me. Had never really been there when I needed him.

Zane, on the other hand, had always been there for me.

And yet he was so, *so* like my dad.

Rock star.

Egomaniac.

Womanizer.

My dad was even badass and blond. At least, he was when he was young.

As soon as I became conscious of the resemblance—at our wedding—it had snaked its way into my bones and taken root, ensnarling me with irritating tendrils of resentment. It was a terrible itch I couldn't scratch, couldn't rid myself of, because—unlike my dad—Zane was always here. In my face. In my life. In everything I did. My employer. My friend.

My worst fear.

No, I most definitely could not trust a cocky manwhore who

treated bedding women like a convenient pastime. Get up in the morning, scratch your ass, have a coffee, go screw someone.

My dad had lived that way, had never put me before the needs of his own libido and his own inflated self-worth, and I did not want another man like that in my heart.

Ever.

But I did, unfortunately, want the rest. The rest of Zane.

A man who was caring, passionate and there for me. A man who would probably *kill* for me.

Sexy. Talented. And yes, a little dangerous.

Just the coolest guy I'd ever met.

That Zane, I knew I wanted.

But you couldn't take one without the rest.

He touched my chin lightly, turning my face back to his. His blue eyes held mine, and there was a challenge in them. "You mean, you can't trust yourself with me."

That was true, too.

And I felt myself shutting down because of it.

"They're in my purse," I told him. "In the zipper on the side. You can go get them and I'll be right there."

"Or I could bring them back in here…"

"Out there," I said. "I wanna dry my hair or I'll get cold."

"I'll keep you warm," he said, sliding his hands down around my ass and squeezing, his fingers biting in deep, sending shivers of lust through every part of me. Then he kissed me again, hot and deep.

I kissed him back, my movements feeling forced, even to me. I could feel myself reeling back in, tucking my emotions back behind my neat and tidy wall—the one Zane had always accused me of putting up between us.

He pulled away, his hooded eyes on mine. Surely, he could feel that wall going up.

He always did.

From his point of view, my wall was probably the root of all our problems.

"I'll meet you out there," he said, giving my ass a final, lingering squeeze. He held my gaze until I nodded.

Then he left, and I took a deep breath.

I turned and pressed my forehead to the tile wall.

I just needed to get some air that wasn't his, some space that he wasn't all pressed up in. A moment to let my body cool down. So I could think straight...

And figure out how to get out of this.

Chapter 3

Zane

There were exactly six of them, in a strip. Ribbed, and the size was XL. Which gave me a wicked surge of satisfaction.

Because clearly, the condoms she'd brought were for me.

Unless Maggie was hoping to have some other dude with an XL dick drill her this weekend…

But fuck that.

If she was, I'd just have to fuck that idea right out of her.

When she came out of the bathroom a few minutes later, I was lying on the bed with the fire burning and the lights out. She stood there in the doorway, looking at me. Her dark hair was half-dried, the ends still damp, and it was smoothed down neatly around her face.

Her body from neck to knee was covered in a hideous army-green thermal that fit her like a tent.

I laughed.

Maggie scowled.

"Wearing another man's shirt again, Maggs?"

She crossed her arms at her waist and I could almost make out her curves. "Jealous?"

"Kinda takes me back. You know, to our wedding night, when you almost fucked Coop before you married me…"

"It's Dylan's," she gritted out. "Because *some* men are thoughtful enough to lend me an extra shirt when I'm helping the staff set up, in the cold. You know, while other men sleep in half the day."

Well, that would explain the fit. Dylan was six-and-a-half feet, a maniac drummer built of solid muscle, and Maggie was about five-foot-nothing and weighed as much as a small bird soaking wet. "That was thoughtful. If he was trying to keep you from getting laid."

"I'm not getting laid."

"Let me guess," I said, sliding my arm behind my head like a pillow. "You've changed your mind."

"It's a woman's prerogative."

"Well, it's a man's prerogative to try again."

She didn't budge from the doorway. "You know, your cabin is way nicer than mine. I know, because I did the rooming assignments. Which is also why it's way the hell on the other side of the resort."

"Geography can't keep us apart, babe."

"Actually, it can. Your dick isn't that long."

I laughed again. "You should've just put us in the same room and saved yourself the trouble."

"Why would I do that?"

"Because you know I'm just gonna end up in here."

"And how do you figure that?"

"Because we're married."

She rolled her eyes. "It's the middle of the night. I wanna go to sleep, Zane."

"So go to sleep. There's room." I glanced down at the bed. It was a double, not huge, but big enough… if I wasn't sprawled across three-quarters of it. "If you can't fit, we can snuggle."

She sighed heavily, walked over, and stood by the bed. She hesitated there, looking at me. Totally fucking unsure.

"Zane. I really don't think we should do this."

"Okay." I moved over to let her in and pulled the sheet over myself. "Hands to myself." I was serious, too. If she really didn't want me to touch her, I wasn't gonna be that guy.

But she'd come around.

She stalled, fussing with the blanket on her side and fluffing up her pillow.

Then she got in the bed. She tucked herself in under the covers, lying stiff as a board on her back, and closed her eyes.

"I mean it," she said. "I'm going to sleep."

"Wouldn't dream of disturbing you," I told her. "I won't even touch you. Promise." Then I took hold of the covers and slowly dragged them off of her.

All of them.

She opened her eyes and looked over at me as I tossed the bedding behind me, on the floor.

I held up my hands. "Not touching you."

"For Christ's sake, Zane. Grow up."

"I'm working on it."

My hand snaked over to her and drew the tent of her shirt up her thigh. Not touching her, just the shirt. Underneath, she'd put on what she probably thought were conservative panties. Plain black ones, like little shorts.

Sexy.

I ran a fingertip along the edge of the panties, over the curve of her hip, the fabric a thin barrier between my skin and hers. "I wonder how hot I can get you without even touching you…"

"Touching my panties counts as touching me, Zane."

"C'mon, Maggie. Where's the fun in that?" I shifted closer to her, and my bare dick poked her in the thigh. By accident. "Does touching you with my dick count?"

She gave me a nasty look. "Zane. I told you. This isn't a good idea, okay?"

I ran my finger back over her panties, and down between her legs, stroking her pussy through the soft fabric. She squirmed, but in a lazy, tired way, like she didn't really have the will to fight—at least, not physically.

As usual, Maggie's body was totally at odds with her stubborn mind.

I slid my hand up and peeled the panties down, carefully, hooking my fingers inside… slipping them slowly down over her hips… my skin never once touching hers.

"Zane…"

"Trust me, Maggie."

She frowned. "Right."

"Okay… so don't trust me. But give me a chance. Two minutes." I slid the panties down her legs and off her feet. "I don't manage to change your mind in two minutes, without touching you, you put your panties and your tent-shirt back on, and I leave you alone."

Then I slipped the shirt up and pulled it off, over her head, with Maggie's semi-cooperation. She flopped naked and half-resistant beneath me, tense and soft, firelit and beautiful.

I put my hands on the bed, on either side of her waist, and leaned down, closer… shifting over her… so close she could feel my breath on her skin. I hovered over one nipple, then the other, as if I might kiss her there, but I didn't.

She arched a little and squirmed beneath me, her breathing getting faster.

Then I moved down… until I was in position to lick her pussy. I didn't. I breathed on her instead, slow and hot, and just let her want it.

When I looked up at her face, she was biting her lip.

"This is ridiculous…" she said. Her tone was bored and tight with contempt, but her words were breathless with need.

And it *was* ridiculous. My speeding heart was ridiculous.

The incessant throbbing of my cock was worse.

I got up and went to the bouquet on the table by the door. I'd already read the card while she dried her hair. It was from Jesse and Katie, thanking her for helping out with the wedding. It was huge, several dozen flowers. I had no idea what they were, but I plucked out one of the big fluffy pink ones with all the fluttery, silky petals. Then I took it back to the bed.

Maggie watched me every step of the way, her eyes wide. She looked so young and sweet and perfect lying there in the firelight, I paused by the bed to look at her. All the hard, accusing lines of her face were softened, her eyes and mouth, usually tight when she looked at me, more relaxed than usual.

I knelt over her on the bed, not touching her at all, and lowered the head of the flower between her legs.

She twisted her full bottom lip in her teeth.

Just before the petals whispered over her clit, I pulled it away. She groaned a little, fisting the sheet beneath her, and my cock jerked.

I just hoped my two minutes were gonna do it.

I drifted the flower over her left breast, spinning it slowly so the petals fluttered over her tight nipple. Then I did the same to the other nipple. Maggie's mouth fell open and her body arched into the light touch—just before I took it away.

Then I fluttered the flower down, down… toward her pussy. I paused, meeting her eyes. She was watching me, and she was losing it. I could see it… her wall was slipping, the way it always did before she gave in to me, before she threw herself right over.

I lowered the flower and fluttered the silky petals over her clit.

Maggie gasped and spread her legs. Her thigh bumped against mine.

"That didn't fucking count," I taunted her, spinning the flower and fluttering it down between her legs. "You touched *me*."

"Zane," she whispered, breathless, "your two minutes are up, okay?" She bucked beneath me as I lifted the flower away.

"You want me to stop?"

"No," she said, pretty much panting. "I don't want you to stop."

A smile spread across my face. I couldn't help it.

I fluttered the flower down again, teasing her… drifting it over her pussy, her inner thighs, as she writhed.

"*Zane*…"

Then I got serious. I got down between her legs and swiped my tongue gently over her sweet flesh, lapping at her clit. Then I drifted the flower over her again. Her hands delved into my hair, trying to hold me down, to make me give her more. She bucked and moaned. But I took my time, holding back… even as it drove me insane. My tongue, the flower… Maggie's cries.

Then my tongue deep inside her… Then the flower whispering over her clit.

Then my mouth on her clit and her cries growing louder.

Her clit tightened under my tongue, her pussy swelling, juicy and wet as my fingertip caressed her opening.

"Do you want me to stop?" I whispered, kissing her pussy, then caressing her with the flower.

"*Do not* fucking stop…"

I got up, and as quickly as I could I slipped a condom on. Then I went back at her… my mouth, the flower… my fingers… Maggie's cries.

When I couldn't take anymore, I moved up her body.

"I know you want me, Maggie," I said, as I kissed her neck. My hand delved between her legs and she bucked against me; her arms flew around my neck and she held me tight. "Why do you fight it so much?" I licked my way up her throat. "You know we're good together..."

"We aren't together," she protested.

"No?" I pushed her thighs farther apart and lowered my hips. I shoved my cock inside her, sliding in deep. She was so wet... she took me, hot and fast. "Sure feels like it to me..."

She moaned, but said nothing.

"I'm gonna fuck you all night if that's what it takes... to get through to you..."

"The night's almost over," she said, breathless, gasping as I rammed into her.

"Then I'll fuck you all morning. You're gonna stay in this room, with me, and you're gonna take my cock, every which way I wanna give it to you... until you see the fucking light..."

Her breathing got rougher as I fucked her, harder, my thrusts gradually picking up speed until she was crying out. I almost lost myself in those ragged, breathy screams of hers...

Music was coming through a wall. Loud. Arctic Monkeys... I wondered vaguely if someone had put it on to drown out Maggie's cries.

At the moment, she didn't seem to give one fuck.

Neither did I.

She was getting close and all I cared about, right now, was getting her there. So I slowed down. Because I knew, with Maggie, that would only get her there faster...

I put my hand on her face, gripping her chin, and made her look at me. "You sure you can handle this?" I challenged her as I looked into her gray eyes... as I pressed her thighs apart with my hips and gave it to her slow. I was almost out of breath as I held myself back, so fucking wrapped up in her I was forgetting to breathe.

"Can you?" she said, peering up at me, her voice just a whisper in the dark.

And the answer was no. I could not handle this.

There wasn't a thing about this I could handle.

The thing about me was… I'd do it anyway.

Chapter 4

Zane

I fucked Maggie right to the edge, and when I felt her tensing up, her nails digging into my ass, her breathing getting all jagged and desperate, I whispered, "What if I can't handle it?"

"What?" Maggie blinked at me, dazed and panting. "What? *Why?*"

"Maggie." I ran the tip of my nose along hers, brushed my mouth against her full lips. "Because I love—"

"NO! No, no." She twisted her head away and tried to push me off. "We need to stop."

So I stopped. I stopped thrusting and just tried to catch my breath.

"I mean *stop,*" she said, shoving at me. "*Pull out.*"

I stared at her. "Are you fucking serious?"

She glared at me.

"Maggie."

"*Zane.*"

"*Christ,* Maggs." I pulled out. "Please tell me you're fucking kidding me," I said, panting, "and you're about to shove me on my back and hop on for a ride. 'Cause I know you love going for a ride."

She scowled at me, also panting, but it was true. Maggie loved being on top. Taking it on her back was not her usual style.

Neither was telling me to pull out seconds before she had a screaming, scorching orgasm.

"If not," I added, "that was about the shittiest thing a chick has ever done to me. And I once had a girl stab me."

"With a hair brush," she said, totally unsympathetic.

"It was sharp."

"I know. Who drove you to the hospital?" She shoved at me again and I sighed, shifting off her as she scrabbled to detach herself from me in every way.

"What's the deal, Maggie?" I fell back on the bed beside her. "You want me. You don't want me. Now you decide you don't want me right in the middle of wanting me? What the fuck."

"What I *want*," she said, still panting, "is to fuck. And you just messed up a totally decent fuck by opening your mouth."

"Yeah? Well, I'm so totally fucking sorry for sharing my feelings with you. I won't do it again."

"Yes, you will. You're *dying* to share your feelings. But news flash, Zane: I am not gonna magically start trusting you just because you tell me you love me."

"Why the hell not?"

"Because you *don't* love me."

We locked eyes like a couple of bulls locking horns, and I wondered if I should take the condom off. My cock was still throbbing, and she just lay there glaring at me, gleaming with sweat in the firelight, her breathing gradually calming, her dark hair fanned out on the pillow.

I propped myself up on an elbow and looked down at her. "And how the hell would you know that?"

"Because," she said, stone-faced, "you don't know the

meaning of the word." But her gray eyes looked soft and vulnerable. She was pissed at me, but she was afraid. That much was obvious.

Maggie and her motherfucking wall.

My gaze trailed down her throat, where her heartbeat thrummed in a frantic rhythm. My hand drifted over, my fingertip tracing a line along her delicate collarbone.

"Is this, by any chance, about Dallas?"

She bristled, her body twitching in protest and her face screwing up like there was a rotten taste in her mouth. But she didn't push me away. "No. It's not about…" She stopped, unable to say the name, apparently, and swallowed. She wouldn't look me in the eye, either. "Women named after cities have enough problems. Who am I to criticize?"

"Uh-huh." My fingertip continued down toward her breast and around the slight swell.

"Or flowers," she went on. "You know, like your little friend Daisy. And what was that other one, in Toronto? Rosie? Or was it Petunia? Who can keep track?" Her tone was cold, but her gray eyes sparked as she finally looked at me.

Fuck me. Maggie, jealous?

Total fucking turn on.

Shouldn't be. I knew that. But my dick never lied to me.

Maggie was hot *as fuck* when she was jealous.

Slowly, I encircled her rosy nipple with my fingertip, and it tightened, rock-hard and begging to be licked. "I never cheated on you, Maggie."

She scoffed.

I held her gray eyes. "You said so yourself. You're not my wife."

"I'm not."

"Well, you can't have it both ways, babe. You're not my wife, then I'm not your husband." My finger slowly circled her nipple again. "And if that's so, doesn't that make my dick a free agent?"

"Your dick can do whatever the fuck it wants," she grumbled.

"Good. Because my dick wants you." I leaned in to flick my tongue over her nipple. As I licked her, she stirred and kind of growled in her throat.

So I took her hand and put it on my dick. I stroked myself with it, slowly, up and down. Then she squeezed her hand around me, vicious-tight. Probably meant to hurt me.

Didn't work.

I looked up at her. "Do you want this or not?" I asked her, my voice low and raspy.

She licked her lip, slowly. "I want your dick." Her gray eyes held mine, cool and controlled. Those eyes that said, *I don't want you.*

But I didn't believe them.

I never did.

So I grabbed her by her hips and flipped her over. She gave up a surprised squeal but she didn't fight.

She didn't tell me to stop.

I straddled her, my knees on either side of her hips, and lifted her ass toward me.

"You want this?" I ran my dick down between her legs, slick against her pussy.

"Yeah," she breathed.

So I rammed myself in. Her hands clawed at the sheet, squeezing it in fistfuls as I sank into her. I leaned down against her, the curve of her back to my front, and ground my hips against her ass. She gasped as she took me, as I forced my way deeper.

I grabbed her neck and held her tight.

"This is all you want?" I asked as she moaned with each thrust.

"*Yes…*"

I fucked her, harder, reaching around to rub her clit with my fingers. Maggie pressed her face into the pillow, shuddering and moaning.

"Then beg for it," I told her.

"*Ung…* Zane," she groaned.

I slammed into her again, and again, until I knew her eyes had to be rolling back in her head.

"Beg me for it."

"No…"

"Fuck, Maggie."

I pulled out. I flipped her over and got between her thighs. Her legs went around me, her arms around my back as I lowered myself on top of her. Then I fucked her the way I wanted to fuck her most; the way that was always hardest to fuck her—face-to-face.

Because, as usual, she evaded that shit.

She buried her face in my neck. She refused to look at me, no matter how I gave it to her. Hard or fast or slow, didn't matter.

She wouldn't look me in the eye.

So I pulled out most of the way, until just the head of my cock was in her, teasing her. Her body protested, her thighs clamping around me, her nails digging into my back.

"Beg me, Maggie," I said.

"*Please*," she spat out.

I gave it to her, hard but not fast, and lifted up a bit so I could see her. So she couldn't hide.

Her eyes were closed. But she was tensing up, her breaths cutting off, shallow and fast.

I leaned down and kissed her neck, licked my way up to her ear. She shivered beneath me.

"If this is all you want…" I whispered as I thrust into her, "then you don't want me to stop… not when you're right on the edge. I can feel it, babe. Know how you feel right before you go off."

She opened her eyes then, just a little, looking at me under her lashes. Those gray eyes... *Christ*, those eyes.

She wasn't the only one riding the edge.

"Say my name, Maggie," I ordered, my voice harsh and ragged.

"Don't—" she said, her breath catching.

"Say it. I wanna hear it when you come."

I pounded into her, slow and deep, snapping my hips up, dragging my pelvis against hers, so she couldn't resist it if she tried. Even if she just lay there and went limp, she'd go off. Because I knew just where to hit her, and how hard, and at what angle, and how many fucking times.

Maybe we hadn't fucked more than a handful of times, but I paid attention.

As she started to come, she said, "*Zane... please...*" and a flare of victory went off in my gut, spreading heat through my insides, even as I shuddered with the force of holding myself back... just waiting for her to go first.

"Yeah, babe..." I held her down as she cried out. As her pussy clenched, choking my cock. As the pleasure rolled through her body... rolled through mine. "I'm gonna fucking blow. Tell me you want it."

Her hazy gray eyes looked up at me. "I want it."

"Fuck... *yeah*... Maggie... I'm gonna give it to you..."

Then I totally fucking lost myself as I blew into her. All I could see was her face. Those gray eyes... just Maggie, gazing up at me, as I gave her everything I had.

Three fucking months of it...

All for her.

———

"Let's tell everyone."

"Tell everyone what?" Maggie looked at me as I collapsed on the bed beside her.

I'd gone to get rid of the condom and discovered my legs were pretty wobbly. Not only had fucking Maggie left me weak in the knees, as usual, but the time of night was really setting in. I was fucking tired.

"You know what," I said, closing my eyes. The idea had hit me in the bathroom, and it was fucking brilliant if you asked me. "We can do it today, at brunch. Our closest friends are here, and there's no media, no internet. Perfect place to tell everyone and ask them to keep it private while we figure our shit out."

"You're kidding me, right?"

I opened my eyes and looked over at her. The firelight flickered on her pretty face, her full lips puckered in an angry pout. She had the sheet all wrapped around her like a cocoon, her head and arms the only bare skin in sight.

"I've never been kidding about this," I told her.

She shook her head, slowly, making an aggravated noise in her throat. The kind that usually got me rock-hard, but all the fighting and fucking at four a.m. had really worn me out.

"Or not," I mumbled, closing my eyes again. So much for that brilliant fucking idea. "It was just a suggestion, Maggs."

"Uh-huh. And let me guess. You came up with it about two seconds ago."

"So?"

"So, you think announcing to everyone, at Jesse and Katie's wedding, that we secretly got married in Vegas almost a year ago, is appropriate?"

"Fuck if I know."

"Zane." She shoved at my shoulder and my eyes cracked open. "We are not doing that to them. This is *their* event, not ours."

"Okay. Whatever."

But Maggie was just ramping up. "Do you have any fucking *clue* how much work went into this wedding? How much they *spent* on it? How many people with other shit to do flew up here, just for them? Because I do. I can tell you what it cost and how much work went into it. *A lot.* Because when people *really* want to get married, that's what they do."

I sighed and closed my eyes. *Here we go again.* "Nice dig, Maggs."

"I can also tell you what it *means* to Jesse and Katie," she went on. "*A lot.*" She poked me in the ribs with her tiny finger. "And since, unlike you, I don't think the entire universe revolves around me and my impulses, I can assure you that despite what you might think, pissing all over their parade with our fucked-up gossip is *not* an appropriate wedding gift. So I really fucking hope you got them something else."

Finally finished, she flopped onto her pillow.

"Of course I did. A pool table." I opened one eye. "You know, so I have something to do at their place when they disappear for a quickie, which they always fucking do."

"So it's a gift for yourself."

I opened the other eye and rolled toward her. "They get to use it when I'm not there."

"That's so thoughtful, Zane."

"I know."

"And anyway, we're not telling anyone about Vegas," she said, not looking at me, "because we are not married."

I sat up, rubbing my eyes. The music next door had suddenly shut off, and the silence was too fucking loud. Didn't realize how loud the music was, actually, until the silence set in.

"Jesus Christ," I muttered. "Enough of this shit." First the wedding, for which I'd endured wearing a fucking suit *and* tie, then the almost two-hour show I'd played after the wedding, many more hours of partying and jamming, a frigid skinny dip, and sex with Maggie—which meant feeling like I'd just gone twelve rounds in a cage match with a feral cat—and I was fucking done. "*Yes*," I told her, "we fucking are."

"Not if we get a divorce."

I leaned down and looked her straight in the eye and told her, just like I already had, several times, "I'm not getting a divorce."

"*Because...?*" she said. "It goes against your principles or something?" Then she scoffed, like I didn't have any.

"Yes. We got married. Let's fucking deal with it already."

She rolled her eyes. And I fucking hated it when she rolled her eyes at me. "You call this a marriage?"

"It could be."

"Just because we had a wedding doesn't mean we have a marriage, Zane."

I rubbed a hand over my face. "So maybe I don't know what the fuck a marriage is. Maybe I don't know *how* to have one."

"Maybe you don't."

"Maybe I wanna try." Was that really so fucking hard for her to believe?

"Well, excuse me if I'm not interested in playing house with you," she said, sitting up abruptly and peeling off the sheet.

"The fuck does that mean?"

I watched her yank on Dylan's giant shirt. Then she tossed me an accusing look. "It means, you wanna run a social experiment in monogamy and commitment, you can do it with someone else."

I stared right back. "So I guess snuggling and pillow talk are out?"

There was a knock at the door and Maggie stiffened. She whispered, "Shut up!"

I didn't even say anything.

"Do not say a word," she hissed, grabbing a pillow and

hugging it, like that could make her disappear. "Do not make a sound." Then she reached over and her hand closed on my wrist.

She looked at me, her gray eyes wide—like the thought of whoever was outside that door seeing me here, with her, was the most appalling thing that could ever happen.

Which rubbed me *way* the fuck wrong. Especially since she'd just come all over my dick.

The knock came again.

Fuck it.

I got up. Because right now, I did not give one shit who was on the other side of that door.

"ZANE," she cried, "DON'T!"

But I did. I went straight to Maggie's door, and I opened it.

Naked.

A Dirty Lie

Author's Note

The night of Jesse and Katie's wedding in *Dirty Like Brody*, we see Jessa Mayes' friend and wedding date, Roni, hauling (naked) ass into the woods after a midnight skinny dip in the frigid waters of Cathedral Cove, accompanied by (naked) Dylan and Ash.

Lucky girl.

Shortly thereafter, Brody thinks he hears Roni "entertaining" both men (loudly) through the wall of Jessa's cabin room.

So, what *actually* happens when sexy "wild card" Roni disappears into the dark with two hot, naked rock stars?

Not what you think…

Jaine

Chapter 1

Roni

"Co—condoms," I wheezed.

My lungs hurt, bad. Well, everything hurt. Because about five minutes ago, a midnight skinny dip seemed like a great idea.

Now? Not so much.

I'd just reached the door to my cabin, but turned around to face Ash and Dylan, who were right behind me, shivering. Both of them watched my naked boobs jiggle as I jumped up and down, trying to get warm. "You've got… condoms?" *Shit.* My teeth were chattering.

"Uh…" Ash glanced at Dylan, then down at his naked self. "Not *on* me." They were both naked, so where they'd carry a condom, I had no idea. But that really wasn't my problem.

All three of us were completely naked, and fucking freezing. The guys were cupping their balls against the cold and dancing from foot-to-foot like some badly-choreographed strip routine. Dylan, big and burly and auburn-haired, and Ash, sleek and edgy and black-haired, muscles and tattoos gleaming in the moonlight. Hot drummer. Hot lead singer.

The stuff girlhood fantasies were made of, right in my face.

Didn't matter. They weren't stepping foot in my room without condoms.

Just because they were crazy-hot rock stars and I'd been flirting with them mercilessly—and them with me—ever since I'd arrived here at the resort, yesterday, for the wedding of Dylan's Dirty bandmate Jesse Mayes, didn't mean I owed them shit. Besides, I learned years ago never to provide the condoms. If a man couldn't make the effort to rustle one up himself, he wasn't worth my fucking time, much less a place in my bed.

If two of them couldn't do it…

"Kinda fucking cold here, Roni," Dylan offered jovially. "Maybe we come in and warm up, then we figure out the condom situation?"

"No dice," I said. "No cover, no lover."

"Hey—*ho*. Sorry."

We all glanced over in unison as Dirty's bass player, Elle, materialized out of the dark, her platinum-blonde hair flashing in the shadows between the trees. She walked right past us, up the boardwalk that connected the various cabins, a tote bag slung over one shoulder, holding up a hand to block her view of the naked guys.

She nodded briefly at me, wearing a small smirk. "Didn't see a thing." She continued on, waving at us over her head, her back to us. "Have a good one, boys and girl."

"*Damn*," Dylan muttered, totally unfazed by the interruption, but slowly absorbing that I was serious. "I'll get the condoms." He gave me a super-quick kiss on the cheek, then dashed off, presumably in the direction of his cabin.

I looked at Ash. Our eyes met, and even in the near-dark, I could see the conflicted expression flicker across his features. A kind of distracted look I'd glimpsed on his face throughout the night. He swiped a hand through his jet-black hair as he bounced on the balls of his feet. I couldn't tell what he was thinking about but, oddly, it didn't seem to be me. Odd since I was standing right in front of him, naked, and presumably, he was about to fuck me.

I opened my mouth to speak but didn't get the chance.

"Me too." He took my hand and kissed it. Then he backed away and took off up the boardwalk.

Okay...?

I hurried into my cabin and straight into the shower, got it scalding hot, and thawed myself out. While I did that, I got a strange feeling. The kind of feeling you had no reason to feel, about things you had no reason to know, and yet you did know.

Ash wasn't coming back.

Pity.

Guess I'll just have to do Dylan twice.

As I got dressed in a flimsy, filmy nightie—with knit leg warmers and a sweater, at least until Dylan got back—I blow-dried my hair on the hottest setting. I'd washed off my wedding makeup in the shower, so I reapplied just a little. Natural yet polished. Fuck-ready.

Then I waited.

As I did, that look on Ash's face came back to me; like he was looking through me, rather than at me. And it started to bother me.

Like *really* bother me.

Five minutes into waiting, I decided *Fuck waiting*.

When had I ever waited around for a man? Even a hot one?

Even *two* hot ones?

Well, there was a time... But that was years ago. And totally didn't count. Everyone was allowed to be a little stupid when they were eighteen.

I was no longer eighteen or stupid when it came to men.

I was more than aware that these ones, in particular, didn't exactly take me seriously; to the boys of Dirty, I was just the wild card. The party girl. That's what they'd called me, ever since I was sixteen, when I met Jesse's sister, Jessa, in high school and we became friends. Roni "Wild Card" Webber. Translation: easy lay. So it hardly surprised me if Dylan, Dirty's drummer, and his best friend, Ash, lead singer of the Penny Pushers, were blowing me off.

Hot as they both were, it was fine by me.

I could blow them off, too.

Dylan was beautiful but really not my thing. Too clean. Too whole. Too... undamaged.

And Ash? I'd met him for the first time at the wedding. I knew who he was, but I'd never really taken notice, per se, until I met him. Smoldering blue eyes, tattoos and piercings and an angsty restlessness just under the skin. Hard to peg. Probably more my style, but I had no idea what his deal was. The guy was hot and cold. Last night at Katie's stagette he was all over me, but then he'd up and disappeared, and Jessa had been so rough—in other words, hard up for Brody, Dirty's manager, but too stubborn to admit it—that she and I had ended up staying up together, drinking until dawn.

And tonight, at the wedding reception... Ash and his general air of distraction had barely even seemed to notice me in my sexy red dress.

Well, fuck it. Waste of time.

And we only got so much time, right? Personally, I had none to waste.

So I got up and I got dressed. I slipped on a g-string and a pair of my skinny, sexy cargo pants, fawn color, with woolly socks and my little hiking boots; totally outdoorsy-chic. I hoisted up the girls in one of my most gravity-defying push-up bras, because I never did anything halfway. Even if no other man laid eyes on me tonight, *I* had to see me, and that totally counted.

People who took one look at me and assumed I dressed the way I did for men assumed *wrong*. I did not need a man—or a hard dick—to make me feel good about myself.

So why did I feel so crappy?

I decided, immediately, not to dwell on that. Evasive action was what was needed here. The frigid cold of that skinny dip had shocked away the totally decent buzz I had going on, and it was time to remedy that. And I just so happened to know where I could find myself a drink.

I layered on a super-low-cut T-shirt, a super-low-cut cashmere sweater, my cute down-filled satin bomber jacket, and walked out the door—and straight into Dylan. All six-and-a-half feet of him. Actually, I plowed face-first into his hard chest.

"Hey," I said, bouncing back.

His wavy auburn hair had mostly dried and he'd gotten dressed. Jeans, cozy sweater, green plaid lumber jacket. Outdoorsy-chic-fucking-delicious.

"Sorry that took so fucking long," he said. "Had no booze left at my cabin. Thought I'd find some in the lodge, struck out. Bar's locked. Ended up raiding a party up at Jude's cabin." He held up two fists, one with a bottle of vodka and the other with a jug of orange juice. "Screwdriver?" He cocked an eyebrow at me and his green-eyed gaze drifted to my mouth as I put on a smile. "Also brought condoms. Studded… for your pleasure."

"I do like a man who's resourceful," I said.

But… *Jude's cabin…*?

I noticed the throb of music in the distance now, muffled through the dense trees, echoing the strange throb of my heart. Unmistakably, it was Nine Inch Nails. "Closer." Heavy, aggressive, fucking sexy song. Yeah; that sounded about right.

Dylan's eyes flicked past me, into my cabin, through the door

I was about to close. "Where's Ash?" Then his gaze scanned slowly down my body, the unspoken question in them: *And why the fuck are you dressed?*

"No idea. But… hey, sorry it didn't work out." I shut the door behind me, firmly.

Dylan lowered the bottles.

"I mean, look, you're sweet…"

His lips quirked in a half-smile. "Ah, shit. Not the 'you're sweet' talk…"

I laughed a little. "Okay. How about this. I like you. Let's be friends?"

"Right. 'Cause I'm sure neither of us have enough of those."

I smiled back, genuinely this time. Dylan Cope had an easy, relaxed charm that was impossible not to smile at. Add to that a killer body he tended to show off in a kilt; I'd even heard he was about to add "underwear model" to his incredibly long list of talents.

So what the fuck was I doing?

Why did it bother me so much that Ash had bailed? Because yeah, it really did.

And not because of Ash.

Because I was on a mission to prove something to myself at this wedding. Well, to myself… and to someone else. Because when Jessa invited me to come as her date, I saw a golden opportunity to indulge my baser self.

Revenge: a dish best served cold…

But apparently, my feelings hadn't run as cold as I'd thought. And now, thanks to Ash bailing on our little threesome, I'd failed to prove shit to anyone, including myself.

Either way, not Dylan's fault.

"No need for sarcasm," I said, cocking my head and flirting just a little. "It's the lowest form of humor, you know."

"Guess I'm just not that funny." With a hooked smile, he hit me with his gorgeous green eyes again. "Anything I can do to change your mind?"

"Unfortunately, no."

"Got it."

He was still standing there, blocking my way. If he was any other guy, I might've just told him to get over it and left him there in the dark. But he really was sweet. And gorgeous.

I wasn't about to tell him that, though. Give him the wrong idea. I'd said the f-word, and if we were gonna be friendly, I couldn't play it both ways.

Nobody liked a tease.

His eyes darkened, like maybe he was reading my mind. Then he leaned in, slowly enough that I could dodge if I wanted to, and kissed me. Slow, and a bit heady-hot, but no tongue. I kissed back, but I held back, too. Way the hell back.

When it ended, he growled a little in his throat, his lips hovering close to mine. "You're a dangerous woman, Roni."

"So I've been told," I whispered.

Then he leaned back, and the moment passed.

"Thanks for not breaking my heart," he added, in what I'd noticed was his lighthearted, easygoing way of handling pretty much everything. Even getting turned down by a potential lover.

"Please." I smoothed out his sweater like a proud mom about to send him off to school. I felt his solid muscles under my hands, his pecs flexing... responsive, willing... eager to please. He watched me do it with hooded eyes.

So maybe the moment hadn't totally passed...

Fuck... he'd be a good lay. Dirty's drummer just had that certain vibe. Pure. Full-steam. All stops pulled.

Like a thoroughbred.

"Think I'm gonna head up to Jude's," he murmured. "You wanna come with?"

"No. Thank you." No fucking way was I going to *that* party. I patted him on the cheek. "Go get laid."

"Yes, ma'am." His eyes sparked with amusement. Then his expression grew serious.

He stepped back and nodded at me, once. It was a nod I'd seen before. The one a guy gave you just before he walked away, to make sure you knew what you'd missed out on. And I did, more or less.

Then he turned and walked away. Just as the darkness was about to swallow him, he paused and held up the vodka. "You wanna keep the drink? Kinda look like you could use it."

"No, thanks. You save it for the girl who's about to blow your mind."

He shook his head. "'Night, Roni," he said, and disappeared.

Well, *fuck*.

That kinda sucked. And yet…

I just wasn't in the mood for a convenience fuck.

And that's all Dylan Cope would've been to me. And me to him.

A wild threesome with two hot rock stars was one thing. Memorable—even to those who weren't involved in it. The kind of thing that got around, even at an event like this. Sure, people were probably hooking up all over this place tonight; what else did you get when you stranded a bunch of hot rock stars and a bunch of women at a remote wedding with an open bar?

But who cared about that?

You wanted people to talk in the morning—you wanted that certain someone from your past to hear about your sexploits—you didn't bang a hot rock star. You banged a hot rock star *and* his best friend, another hot rock star, at the same time. Then at least you got an honorable mention over morning brunch.

Shit. Was that really what this was all about?

And if so… when had I become so lame?

I could see now, since the buzz had worn off and the hot, naked distractions had evaporated into the night, that that was a really stupid reason to fuck someone. Or two someones.

But truth be told, I'd fucked a man for stupider reasons. Like, for instance, thinking I was in love with him. Or worse…

Thinking he was in love with me.

I took a breath of the amazingly fresh night air and told myself to let it go. Just forget about it.

Nobody cares.

Neither should you.

I started around the deck, heading away from the music that surely led to Jude's cabin. Away from the direction both Ash and Dylan had disappeared. Just trying to get present in the moment and absorb my surroundings, because this place deserved nothing less.

Rainforest on the Pacific coast, with ancient, towering trees and water crashing on the rocks below. It was crisp-cold tonight, the resort notched into a cove off the dark ocean, secluded. No snow. Just riding that edge of frozen, everything chilled and green and ready to unfurl in spring.

Winter paradise.

The sun would be up in a few hours; I could probably just wander around all night, fall asleep under the stars. Maybe curl up on one of the couches on the wraparound deck of the lodge with a couple of blankets.

And a nightcap. A toast to me and my lack of any need for a man. Just enjoy my own company for a while.

Because it really didn't matter what anyone else thought or said about me, good or bad, in the morning.

Since when the hell did I care what anyone had to say about my sex life anyway?

Chapter 2

Roni

As I walked past Jessa's room, I noticed her light was on and I stopped. I thought about knocking on her door, maybe staying up all night chatting like we did last night, but decided against it. Tonight, I really didn't mind being alone.

But just then, the door opened.

And Brody stormed out.

Tall, dark and broody Brody Mason, Dirty's manager and the guy Jessa, apparently, had it super fucking bad for. Not that she'd said as much to me. She didn't have to.

"Roni," he growled as he shut the door behind himself. He looked frazzled as he clawed a hand through his hair; wound up.

Recently fucked?

No. Definitely not. Way too much tension rolling off him for that.

"Hey," I said, wondering if I should check on Jessa after he left.

"I was just gonna knock on your door," he said abruptly. "Jessa's in the bath. Can you look in on her? She's drunk."

"Oh. Sure."

"Good." Then he stormed off, just like that.

Hmmm…

I went in and knocked on the bathroom door. I could hear what sounded like weeping. *Great.* I'd never been good with weepers. And Jessa Mayes had always been one. Lucky for me, she didn't often get weepy with me. "Babe. You okay?"

"Roni?" Sniffles and a little splash. She was still in the tub.

"Yup. Should I come in?" *Please say no.*

"No. I'm okay. I'll be out in a bit. Can you stay?"

"Yeah." I sighed. "I can stay."

I grabbed a tiny bottle of Baileys from her mini fridge, opened it and sipped. Then I flopped onto her couch, zoning out to the tunes she had playing. Arctic Monkeys. Some depressing thing about crawling back to someone when you've had too much to drink…

Just a little too fucking fitting for my liking.

I turned it off.

A few minutes later Brody stormed back in, tossed some black fabric thing at the couch, and left again. It hit my boot and plopped on the floor.

What the hell was that about?

I picked it up. Some old Led Zeppelin T-shirt.

When Jessa finally emerged from the bathroom, she looked a wreck. Her eyes were puffy and bloodshot from boozing and crying.

"Wow," I remarked. "Good thing you don't have a photo shoot tomorrow. You'd be incredibly fired."

Despite her current appearance, Jessa was a model, but she'd never been stuck up about it. She giggled all bubbly, like baby Dumbo after he'd gotten smashed in a bucket of booze in that old Disney cartoon. "Thanks." Then she blinked at the Zeppelin shirt

I'd draped on the back of the couch, seeming to sober a bit, and glanced forlornly at the door. "Is he gone?"

"Does it look like he's here?"

She hugged herself and didn't answer.

I steered her over to a chair and sat her ass down, and blow-dried her hair. Then I tucked her into bed.

"You're amazing, Roni," she gushed as she cuddled into her pillow.

So, yeah. Pretty drunk.

"You okay?" I smoothed her hair back from her face. "You want me to find him, ask him to come back?"

She blinked up at me with her big brown eyes. "Why?"

"You tell me."

"Yeah…" she said. Then, "No." And about three seconds later, she was asleep.

———

I waited a few minutes to be sure Jessa was out. Then I got the hell out of there and knocked on the door to Maggie's room, next door.

There was only so much nurturing I could handle, and I'd just maxed out my annual quota when I brushed another woman's hair. But as Dirty's assistant manager, Maggie was probably used to handling other women's hair—like holding it out of toilet bowls while they puked and stuff. Much more suited to this gig.

There was a fire burning in her room; I could see it through the window curtain. But no movement, no noise.

I knocked again. Maybe she was asleep. Or—?

"ZANE, DON'T!"

I heard some footsteps, then the door opened and I glimpsed Maggie, sitting on the bed across the room. She was hugging a pillow. And there was Zane Traynor, lead singer of Dirty, the gorgeous golden god of rock, in my face.

Naked.

He smirked when he saw me and leaned casually on the door frame, as if his legendary cock wasn't hanging out. "Wild card," he said. "How's it hangin'?"

I glanced down because I couldn't really help it, given that question. Impressive, sure, but I wasn't impressed. I was aware that Jessa had assumed Zane was the reason I'd wanted to come to this wedding with her. But she was wrong about that.

Way wrong.

"Not bad," I said, unfazed.

When I looked at Maggie again, she was covering her face. I heard muffled swearing into the pillow.

Zane's gaze crept down to my cleavage, his smirk widening into a grin. "Yeah? Dylan and Ash treating you well?"

Maggie exploded out of bed. "Don't answer that. It's none of his *business*." She grabbed the door from Zane's grasp, elbowing him aside. "How are you?" she asked me, with way too much enthusiasm for this time of night. Up close, she looked a wreck. She was wearing the ugliest tent of a puke-green shirt, with no pants, and her hair was all messed up. I'd never seen the girl with a hair out of place.

Actually, she looked fucked.

I knew what a well-fucked woman looked like.

"Uh… okay," I said. "I was wondering if you could pop in and check on Jessa? You know, make sure she's still breathing? She's been sucking back booze like a sorority girl and she's passed out now, but I wanted to go for a walk. I mean, if you're not busy…" I glanced at Zane, who was still grinning.

"Yeah. For sure," Maggie said. Again, too much enthusiasm. "We're up. I'm up. We were just talking. Zane was helping me with something. We can check on her. I can check on her. I can go stay with her. Because I'm not staying here. I mean, this is my room. He's not staying…"

Her awkward babbling trailed off. I didn't know Maggie well enough to know if this kind of babbling was normal for her or not, but it definitely didn't seem healthy to spew out so many words without breathing.

"Okay," I said when she seemed finished. "Thanks."

Then I walked away.

I heard Zane laugh and Maggie swear as she shut the door.

No idea what that was about, but at least everyone except me was getting laid tonight. And I happened to know for a fact that Zane Traynor was an amazing lay.

So kudos, Maggie.

At least, he *was* an amazing lay five years ago… back when I was twenty-one and screwing rock stars seemed like the world's best idea.

Especially if they were friends with Jude Grayson.

———

The lodge was faintly aglow in the night, its wraparound deck rimmed with golden lanterns, the chandeliers inside the windows dimmed, a fire burning low in the hearth. Everything else was dark, still and silent as I approached. I didn't see a single other person around. Even the staff had cleared out.

Perfect.

I found one of the glass doors along the deck unlocked and slipped it open, stepping inside.

Dylan said the bar was locked, but I'd made a point of flirting with the bartender at the wedding reception and found out where he kept the key. Not that he'd told me; I'd watched him stash it in a drawer. You just never knew when information like that might come in handy, right?

I headed straight for the bar, across the grand room.

And that's when I saw him.

A man, sitting alone in front of the fireplace, on a small love seat facing the fire. I saw his dark head of hair tipped back, resting against the back. Sleeping, maybe. Hopefully.

I'd just have to slip out before he saw me...

But as I neared the bar, the side of his face came into view... that unmistakable face.

It was *Jude.*

Of all fucking people.

Jesse's best man. Dirty's head of security.

The worst mistake of my life.

His big body came into view. And *big* was definitely the word. He was lounged back on the love seat, thighs spread wide, and I saw it.

I saw it *all.*

I stopped short... and it took me a delayed moment to process what I was seeing.

I was seeing Jude's dick.

He had his dark T-shirt shoved up, showing his thick, washboard abs, his sweats shoved down to expose himself, and his long, swollen dick was in his hand.

He was *jerking off.*

I glanced around, but there was no one else here. I half-expected some hot young bimbo to come crawling out from behind the couch at any moment.

But no. There was no one but him.

And now, me.

I couldn't tell if his eyes were closed, but his dark eyelashes were lowered. His heavily-tattooed arm flexed as he pumped. His mouth was open a bit and I could hear him breathing, low and strained, as he worked himself...

And heat crashed through me in a wave.

I swallowed.

Well… There was something I never thought I'd see again.

I just stood there, staring. Wanting to laugh, wanting to run, wanting to strut right over and lend him a hand… all in equal measure. Instead, I did something else.

I started singing, loudly.

"HEEEYYYYY JUDE—"

"Fuck!" He sat up like a shot. "Jesus! Don't sing the fuckin' song."

I laughed. I fucking *howled* with laughter. "You should see your fucking face!"

"Shit. She sings me the fuckin' Beatles while I've got my cock in my hand." In no particular hurry, he wrestled his hard dick into his sweats, which tented rudely. "You think I haven't heard that song enough in my goddamn life?"

"So blame your parents."

"I do. Fuckin' hippies." He swiped a hand through his thick, almost-black hair and fell back on the couch, heaving out a sigh. "And now she's talkin' to me about my parents. Christ."

I was still laughing, doubled-over. Actually, I was crying. Tears leaked out the corners of my eyes, shimmering in the firelight. He was getting blurry, but I could still see him scowling at me.

"Wow. Oh, shit. I haven't laughed like that… Well, since the stagette last night." I wiped the tears away.

"So fuckin' glad I could provide your nightly amusement."

"Oh, don't pout." I stood up tall and crossed my arms under my chest. "It's so pathetic when men pout. And please, don't let me stop you." Against my better judgment, I sauntered over and perched on the arm of the love seat, totally fucking in love with the fact that I'd caught him in a vulnerable moment, even if it barely fazed him. Because clearly, it didn't.

Despite the fact that he'd put his dick away—more or less—

his sweats were still riding so low I could see the shadow of his closely-shaven treasure trail, his shirt still halfway up his abs as he lounged back. The man was dead fucking sexy. Sexist man I'd ever…

But I didn't plan on letting that faze me, either.

"Please, carry on. I wouldn't dream of leaving a man hanging."

Well, tell that to Dylan…

"I'm good," he said, but his cock didn't look any less put out. I could see the thick head clearly outlined as it pressed against the fabric of his dark sweats.

Damn…

Jude had a monster dick when he was twenty-one. Guess that hadn't changed. In my fantasies of him over the years, it definitely had; like maybe he'd started doing 'roids to pump up his hot bod, and his dick had shrunk to the size of a raisin, and his life had fallen apart.

Yeah; those kinds of fantasies.

I met his eyes. Dark and smoldering and totally fucking dangerous.

So those hadn't changed, either.

Jude had been hot back then, but now he had a monster body to go with his dick, and he'd really grown into his rugged-gorgeous looks. Had a lot more tattoos, too. He pretty much lived the life of a rock star, managing security for one of the biggest bands in the world, working alongside his best friends, and if that wasn't enough, he was a patched member of a powerful outlaw motorcycle club, alongside his brother. All of which meant that he had big, fat bank and pretty much his pick of any pussy that drifted his way.

So no, Jude's life hadn't fallen apart. More likely every boyhood fantasy he'd ever had had come true.

Because life was fair like that.

"May I ask why you're jerking off?" I inquired, busting his balls a bit. "You know there are women here, right?"

He shrugged a shoulder but the look in his eyes, which were still fixed on me, was not casual. It was sex-hazed, rough and ready. "Just felt like it." He shifted over a bit, his gaze dropping to linger on my breasts, so purposefully I couldn't even pretend not to notice. He patted the seat cushion next to him. "Have a seat."

Right.

There were about five inches between him and the end of the tiny love seat, and my ass was not that small. And I definitely wasn't sitting on that monster in his lap. Even though, clearly, he was offering it up... as he spread his thighs a little wider, his arm tossed up on the back of the love seat. Casual, not casual. Just putting it out there to see if I'd bite.

And I had to wonder... If another woman had happened to walk in on him while he had his cock out, and she had her cleavage out, would he have asked her to sit down, too?

Yes.

Well, maybe.

"I'm good," I said.

I started to get up, but then paused. I looked at him just sitting there, staring at me.

I sat back down.

"You wanna smoke a joint?" I pulled one from the pocket of my jacket. "I was just going to."

Stupid.

Actually... really, *really* stupid.

When the hell had I become so stupid?

When he didn't answer right away, I got up to leave for real. Like I really didn't give one fuck. I was just being polite, right?

"I'm on duty," he said. His tone was serious, but it was hard to take him seriously when his dick was still up.

I started backing away as I spoke. "So... you'll jack off on duty, but you won't smoke up?"

The barest hint of a smirk curved his full lips. "Man's gotta have his ethics."

"Suit yourself." I turned away before his dimples could make an appearance and I got even more stupid. But as I walked away, I could *feel* his eyes all over my ass.

"*Roni.*"

I stopped, my heart thudding in my chest at the sound of my name in that low, soft growl.

"I'm just messin' with you, darlin'."

Jesus. Darlin' was it, now?

I turned back.

"You know," I mused, "being 'on duty' never would've stopped you before. I remember you, twenty years old, working with the band…" *Shit.* What was I doing now? Flirting? "Just a lowly roadie back then, bouncing parties and hauling gear, but partying as hard as anyone else." Yeah. I was totally flirting. "Harder, I bet."

He stared at me with that look in his eyes.

Hellfire.

Jude's eyes had always reminded me of hellfire. A deep, molten brown that burned right into you. It wasn't a stare that looked through you, to all the other women you could've been but weren't… like Ash's did.

Jude looked at me like he really saw me.

He'd always looked at me like that.

"I remember you, too," he said.

And with that, I should've turned and walked away. Just left things on that high note.

Instead, I kept flirting.

Because old habits die hard.

"So now it's all work and no play for poor Jude?"

He cracked a rare smile, the deep dimples flashing in his

cheeks. And I felt the tiniest surge of victory—even as that smile hit me, right between the legs. "I play when I want to."

"And?" I challenged. "Can't some of your boys take over? I don't see any imminent security threats around here."

"My boys are off for the night. Having a party in my cabin. That's the thing about boys…" His eyes roamed down my body as he spoke. "Gotta let 'em blow off steam sometime."

I planted my hand on my cocked hip and perused the scene. "So… you escaped to blow off some steam of your own, in front of a crackling fire?"

He raised a dark eyebrow, his dimples still on display. "You laughin' at me, V?"

I stared at him, my heart beating a little too hard in my chest.

He called me V.

Which gave me a very unexpected—and yes, stupid—surge of hope that he still had a soft spot for me?

Well, not that he ever really did. Not exactly.

More like a hard spot…

"No," I said. "It's very romantic, Jude." I made sure to look deep in his hellfire eyes and hold his gaze when I said, "I just never thought of you that way. You know, as a romantic."

Then I turned and walked away, in no particular hurry, giving him ample time to appreciate my ass in my tight cargos… and ponder what he'd been missing.

"*V*," he said.

And I couldn't resist. I stopped and turned back to him, again.

He gestured at his crotch, at the stiff bulge of his cock in his sweats. "Just gotta give me a minute here, darlin'."

"Uh-huh." I turned on my heel. "There's a key for the bar cabinets in the drawer by the sink," I told him over my shoulder as I walked away. "I like tequila."

"I know you do," he said, and I could hear the smile in his voice as I walked out the door.

Chapter 3

Jude

Roni. Fucking Veronica Webber.

Blast from the fucking past.

I tried not to think about that. Thought, instead, about how bad Dylan's shoes stank after playing drums all night, all the times I'd walked into some shared bathroom on the road that reeked of puke... the time me and Brody had to pick broken glass out of a nasty gash on Zane's ass...

Yeah, that worked.

Once my cock was down, I threw on my hoodie and got that key. I swiped a couple of shot glasses and a bottle of tequila. Then I went to the door and looked outside. Watched her standing there against the deck railing, her profile to me as she looked out over the dark water below.

Glad I didn't say anything ridiculous while all my blood was in my dick.

Yeah, so I'd pretty much offered up my cock, when I was hard as fuck and she was sitting right there, still laughing at me. But that was all horny bullshit and bravado.

Truth was, a woman with Roni's talents deserved better than a quick fuck. And quick was what it would've been. Was about ten seconds from blowing my load when she interrupted me.

And glad she did.

Been a lot of girls in and out of my life. My bed. Was like that for a lot of guys I knew in the rock 'n' roll life. In the MC life. But for some guys, lucky or unlucky, there was that one girl you remembered, different from all the rest. The one you sometimes thought about out of the blue, no matter how long it'd been since you last had her. And you wondered, *Would she be that fine if I had her again?* Because she was that epic.

Sexy, obviously.

Pretty.

Had some other qualities like a big, infectious laugh and a lack of self-consciousness, a freeness you could admire and didn't see a lot in other women.

And something else. Something you couldn't put your finger on, and maybe that was the attraction. That unknown quality that worked its way under your skin and stayed with you.

That something different.

More than just the taste of her or the wild noises she made. The feel of her, naked and soft, against your skin... How hot and wet her pussy was. How tight her ass was. How good she sucked you off.

It wasn't just fucking her.

It wasn't just her fucking you.

More.

Some crazy head-spinning shit, some kind of magic you made as your bodies slammed together.

As I watched her standing there, the curve of her slightly arched back as she leaned on the rail, the way her pants hugged her round ass, the way her thick, black hair hung down her back and framed the side of her face, I remembered it. Like a tug in my stomach. Lower… like a pull.

Like a tiny blade twisting when she looked over. Just one of her bright green eyes glittering at me.

Come the fuck over here, that eye said.

I opened the door. Went to her and poured her a shot. She sparked up her joint and passed it to me.

"You roll this fatty?" I asked, impressed.

"It's a talent."

I offered it back. "Ladies first."

She shook her head. "I insist."

So I took a drag and passed it back. I poured myself a shot. Then we clinked glasses and she said, "To good times."

"To epic times," I said, and we shot back the liquid gold.

She smiled, but it was a guarded smile, like she hadn't decided if she was happy or not. "How was it?" she asked.

"How was what?" I leaned against the railing next to her.

"You know." She flicked an eyebrow toward the lodge. "In there. You see stars? Or was it more of a utilitarian wank?"

I chuckled. "Come again?"

"Your tug fest," she said, and took a drag on the joint. "What kind of orgasm was it?"

"The nonexistent kind."

Now she raised her eyebrow at me. "I thought you finished."

I laughed again. "While you're out here waitin' on me?" I took the joint as she passed it back and took a drag.

"You took long enough."

I let my gaze drift down her open jacket, her low-cut shirt. I could see the full curves of her juicy tits, mocking me. "What can I say? You look good in cargos." I watched as she poured us both another shot. "Took a while to cool off."

"That's very sweet," she said, like it wasn't sweet at all. "But it wasn't my cargos that got you there. So you don't need to loop me into it. I'm not that fragile."

"Never thought you were." A lock of her black hair had fallen across her cheek. I reached up and smoothed it back from her face so I could see those green eyes. "Was definitely your cargos that would've finished it off, though."

She smiled a little, again, but in that flippant way that meant she didn't believe me. She raised her shot in toast. "To... even better times? Whatever's better than epic." She cocked her head at me. "Is there such a thing?" And as usual, I couldn't tell if she was flirting with me or mocking me. Teasing me, just because she could.

"To the best times," I said.

We clinked and shot the booze back.

I handed her the joint. She looked down over the water and leaned over the rail as she smoked. I watched her dark hair dance in the slight breeze. Let my gaze wander down the curve of her back, to that round, tight ass. To the hit of memory: Roni bent over in front of me, my hands digging into her hips, that sleek arch of her naked back, gleaming with sweat.

I looked away, out over the water.

"This place is insane," she said with a small sigh.

"Yup."

I leaned farther over the rail, just like her, to see her face. There was a sweet, dreamy look on it as she took another drag on the joint, then handed it to me.

"You gonna invite me when you get married here someday?" I asked her.

Roni stared at me. Then she looked out over the water again, her gaze unfocused like she wasn't really seeing it. "A young man told me, years ago, that I'm not the marrying kind."

I took a slow drag off the joint, thinking about that. "Must've been a real douche. And you listened to that shit?"

"No. I never really listened to any of the shit you said. You said a lot of shit back then."

True enough.

"Did piss me off for a while," she admitted.

"You still pissed, darlin'?"

She poured us another shot. "I'm here, aren't I?" Those unreadable green eyes held mine. "Besides, I don't really do pissed anymore. Pissed implies attachment to outcomes, and I don't have those. Cheers."

This time, we drank without toasting anything.

"No?" I licked tequila from my lips. Despite the cold, my insides were growing warm.

"Nope."

"Never?"

"Not usually."

"How 'bout tonight?" I asked, handing the joint back to her. Because I saw her at the wedding reception in that sexy-as-fuck red dress, looking like a five-alarm fire, waiting on Ash to notice. "You got outcomes for tonight?"

"Nope," she said.

"Ashley Player not an outcome, then?"

She looked out over the water again as she smoked. "Nope."

I shifted closer to her and nudged her shoulder, lightly. "Thought you were lookin' to hook up with him tonight."

She looked at me, not quite turning her head, just glancing around the curve of her hair. Then she smiled, just a little, her green eyes sparkling. Girl could play a tough game.

Hardest chick to read I'd ever met.

"Dylan, too," I added.

She passed me the joint. "Is that what it looks like?"

"Looked like. Actually, you ask me, looked like pussy purring up the wrong tree."

She laughed. "Excuse me? Pussy what now?"

"Ash," I said. "Kid's mind is somewhere else."

"I noticed." She poured us another shot and handed one to me. "You wanna tell me where?"

"Nope. Not my place."

We clinked and drank.

"And now?" she asked, looking out over the water again as she licked tequila from her lip. "Where's my pussy purring?"

My gaze lingered on her plump lips, flushed and moist from tequila. I stared so long she finally turned to look at me, and her eyes met mine.

I raised the joint to her lips and held it for her, while she gave it a little suck.

"Up to you, V."

She just looked at me as she exhaled smoke.

"The way I see it," I added, "you could be with Dylan or Ash right now. But you aren't. And in my experience, darlin', when you're choosing between two options, even two good ones, there's always a third."

"Hmm," she said, like that was mildly interesting.

But she didn't ask what that third option was.

I took a long, deep pull off the joint, filling my mouth with smoke but not breathing it in. Then I let my gaze trail down her face again, to those swollen, cocksucking lips.

"C'mere," I murmured.

She didn't come, but she didn't pull away when I leaned in. Her lips parted, and I fit my mouth to hers, almost… never quite touching her lips as I breathed the smoke into her mouth.

She breathed it in.

Then my lips brushed hers, lightly, hovering.

She drew away an inch.

"You still call me V," she said softly. Her eyes were soft, too. Maybe the pot going to her head.

"Your name, isn't it?" I licked my lip without meaning to. "Fucking Veronica."

"Yeah," she said. "No one else seems to remember it." Then she moved to pour us another shot.

I stopped her. "No more booze."

She glanced at me, then looked away, letting the bottle go. I set it aside. I watched her watch the water rush over the rocks below.

"You don't like Roni?"

"Roni's good," she said.

I took a drag from what was left of the joint, considering. "You don't like it when the boys call you wild card."

"Fuck, no. They might as well call me slutbag and get it over with. For a bunch of rock stars, they're a bunch of fucking prudes."

I chuckled. "Slutbag would be a compliment. Trust me. They mean wild card as one."

"No, they don't."

"You'd be surprised."

She raised an eyebrow and I leaned in closer to her.

"Brats on a playground. They're all jealous of what they don't have. Shiny toys… All the boys want 'em, even if they're not supposed to."

She smiled a little. "Did you just call me a toy?"

"Not if you didn't like it."

She smiled again. A genuine smile, for once. It lit up her face, her cheeks kinda glowing in the cold. But those green eyes were still wary.

"How 'bout me?" I asked casually. "Am I a prude?"

"You were never a prude. Just… selective."

"That right?" I looked down, watching the waves lick the rocks below. Dropped the roach into them, watched the ember sparkle down and snuff out. "Did I mention you look good in those cargos?" I turned my body to face her, letting my gaze move slowly down her curves. "Looked good in that red dress, too."

"Didn't know you noticed."

"Notice a lot of things, darlin'."

She turned to me, her gaze drifting down my body. "So do I."

I was hard in my sweats, again, and I knew she could tell. No way I could hide a hard-on this size, even in the near-dark.

She looked up at me and I saw the options there, flickering behind her eyes.

Go back to her cabin, alone.

Wander the woods the rest of the night, alone.

But there was always that third option…

"So…" I asked her, "you gonna play nice, V? Or make me work for it?"

Her eyes narrowed a little as she considered that.

"I never play nice." She glanced at my cock again before meeting my eyes. "But why don't you take it out, and *I'll* do the work."

Chapter 4

Roni

I t was just too fucking sweet to resist.

The ultimate revenge.

As Jude pushed the front of his sweats down, baring his big dick... hard... so totally fucking hard and swollen, for me... I'd never felt anything like the rush of it. I watched him jerk, tightening in anticipation, swelling even more as he waited for it. As he thought about what I was about to do.

Yeah... hard, swollen, straining revenge, just aching for my attention. What could possibly be better than the man who'd once rejected you wanting you again?

I could've walked away from him right then, just to rub it in.

But where was the fun in that?

There was no higher high, nothing I'd ever felt that was better, more delicious, more intensely arousing and at the same time totally fucking *gratifying* than the sensation of getting on my knees in front of that big, hard dick... and taking a taste of him.

Slowly.

While he groaned.

While he shifted and stirred and put his hands in my hair. Just lightly.

Shit. He was being sweet with me. And that, I didn't expect.

I couldn't blame him for taking my mouth when I offered it. But he didn't have to be sweet about it. He didn't have to be gentle with his hands, as he held my head and let me take control.

He could've been a total fucking cocky asshole about it.

But then again, Jude had never been an asshole.

And as I teased his fat cockhead with a slow, torturous lick, and flickered the tip of my tongue over his slit, tasting that delicious taste, that first drop of his salty fluid… it hit me, hard. Made my head spin with the question…

Who was really in control here?

I took him then, fast, not bothering with the slow buildup, the tease. I just stroked my tongue along his shaft, once, to get him wet, then took him deep, making him groan again. I sucked him off, hard and fast, wrapping one hand around the base of his cock and squeezing hard, strangling him, the way I knew he liked it back then, cupping his balls and tugging with the other hand.

"*Jesus Christ, V…*" he growled.

Then he pulled away, ripping his dick from my mouth.

I looked up at him. We were both panting.

He cupped my face and held my eyes. "You gonna make my night or what?" he asked, stroking a thumb lightly down my cheek.

"Was just about to," I said, swiping my tongue over my lip, still tasting him.

"Not what I meant."

He pulled me to my feet. Then he cupped my face again. He leaned in, and as his mouth met mine, it was foreign and so familiar… like being kissed by a stranger and someone you knew like the palm of your own hand—someone you'd kissed a thousand times in your dreams, or on the edge of sleep, half-conscious as your hands roamed over your own body… as you got yourself off to the half-remembered smell of him, the slippery fullness of his lips, the slight roughness of his stubble, the soft scrape of his teeth against your skin.

I broke away, drawing back for air.

He stared at me.

Then he caught my hand. He drew me with him, moving toward the lodge.

And I went with him, letting him take me there.

Inside, he walked me over to the little love seat and stood me right in front of it, close to the fire, and said, "Take off your clothes."

Then he sat down in the middle of the seat, watching me.

"Don't you wanna do it for me?" I asked, still catching my breath.

"I want to watch," he said.

So be it.

I got undressed, and I did it slowly. I started with my jacket. My boots, then my socks. My sweater went next, peeled slowly over my head and tossed aside. My T-shirt, then my jeans. Every zipper pulled slowly, every button popped with a slight pause. Watching his eyes grow darker as he drank in the curves of my body, all rimmed in firelight.

I unhooked my bra and let it slide loose down my arms, holding it in front of me, teasing him a little before I dropped it.

My panties went next in a slow, slow peel.

As soon as I was naked, he got up and prowled the two paces it took to get right in my face. He raised one hand to my breast and cupped lightly, skimming his thumb over my nipple as it hardened in response.

A delicious, tingling shiver ran through me.

And… *no*. This was not just about revenge.

I knew it as he leaned so close to me that I could feel his heat, could smell his clean, manly smell, could feel the hairs on his arm dusting my skin... and my whole body wound up tight with anticipation—even as I held back.

This was about me—getting what I wanted. What I'd *always* wanted, if I was at all honest with myself about it.

Namely, the dark-haired beauty, the beast right in front of me.

He leaned down to touch his lips to my neck, breathing in my ear. "Get on your back," he murmured. I shivered again as his lips skimmed along my jaw and briefly hovered over my mouth.

I kissed him then, softly, my lips just catching his, making him pause. The feel of him, the heat of him, went straight between my legs. I felt giddy-hot and restless with need. I sucked a bit on his bottom lip, before he drew back.

His hellfire eyes flashed at me.

"On your back," he said.

"I wanna get you off," I whispered.

"You will." He leaned in and skimmed his lips across my cheek, to my ear again. "I want you on your back," he said, his teeth catching on my earlobe. My pussy throbbed... ached as he bit down, lightly. "Wanna hold you down and give it to you, while you beg me for more."

Not gonna happen.

That's what I would've said to any other man.

To him, I just said, "Where?"

"Wherever you want."

I looked around. The love seat was too small for both of us, if he wanted me on my back. Otherwise, there were no full-sized couches, just chairs.

Of course, there was always the floor...

But I went over to the love seat and climbed up onto the velvety upholstered back. I reclined back on it, keeping myself propped up on my elbows, for now, so I could watch him as he lost his hoodie, kicked off his shoes and pulled his shirt over his head, then stripped off his socks and sweats. He wasn't wearing underwear.

When my gaze landed on his naked cock, it hit me.

"Oh, *shit*. Condom," I said, sitting up.

"I have some." He reached for his hoodie and dug around in the pockets, and I snickered a bit.

"You always carry condoms when you jerk off?"

He smirked. "Always come prepared."

"What is that, some Boy Scouts thing?" I teased.

"It's a smart thing," he said, his gaze roaming down my naked body, "obviously."

I put my feet up on the back of the love seat, my knees bent, pointed my toes and arched my back, like a pinup. "Well, come and get it then," I said, as he rolled a condom over his hard length.

"Intend to."

Naked and totally fucking gorgeous, he stalked over to me. I lay back as he lifted my legs. Without hesitation, he straddled the back of the love seat, one foot on the seat and the other on the floor, and wrapped my legs around his waist. Then he notched the swollen head of his cock into my pussy. I was already wet and ready to take him; I braced for his thrust as my heart hammered in my chest.

But he hesitated. "You want foreplay, darlin'?" he asked me. "'Cause that look on your face says you don't."

"Fuck foreplay," I said.

He smirked a little. He ran his hands up my body and cupped my breasts, squeezing hard... then he shifted his hips forward, sliding into me.

And *God*... that feeling.

Cock.

Big cock.

Jude's cock...

It fucking *shattered* me.

This. God, I wanted this…

I writhed, arching my back as I took him, as he stretched me to my limits with that long, slow push…

He didn't let up until he'd filled me. Then he paused, closing his eyes as he took a breath, savoring the feeling.

And my stomach twirled. My chest tightened. A whole lot of unfamiliar, fucking disturbing feelings ripped through me as I stared at his face.

He opened his eyes, locking on mine, and pulled back… then shoved into me again, still squeezing my breasts. Harder this time. Faster.

And I just tried to hold still.

To keep calm.

He shoved into me again and again as I lay there on my back, my thighs wrapped around his hips, gripping the love seat beneath me with both hands. Not because I was afraid of falling off. Jude would never let me fall.

Because I didn't want to touch him with my hands.

I didn't want to feel his warm, silky skin and the bulge of his muscles beneath, flexing as he drove into me. I didn't want to pinch and tease his rigid nipples and hear him growl.

Most of all, I didn't want to grab him and pull him down to me so I could kiss him again.

If I did that, I was gonna lose it. Start whimpering and panting and making a total fucking fuss that I couldn't take back. Jude's face in my face, his mouth on me again… I just couldn't fucking stand it while his cock was inside me. I *knew* I couldn't.

He fucked me harder, but slowing right down, gripping my breasts to hold me where he wanted me while his hips did the rest. He swiveled them as he dug in, working the head of his cock against my front wall—studying me the entire time, even as I lay still.

Then he slammed his pelvic bone against my clit.

I cried out. I couldn't help it.

And a slow, wicked smile transformed the dark, controlled look on his face. His dimples flashed.

I closed my eyes.

Because I'd just flashed forward. To the moment when this ended. When he pulled out… and walked away.

And I got a serious lump in my throat.

I covered it all by throwing my head back and letting myself go a little, moaning as he gave it to me, letting the heat and friction and longing build inside me, even as my throat got tight and my heartbeats sped up.

Would he walk away? Right after this?

Yes.

But how fast would he do it?

And how much would it hurt?

Shit. Just… *shit.*

Since when was I afraid of casual sex?

There were always more trees to purr up, right?

But Jude… Jude was different.

Shouldn't be, but he totally was.

There was nothing about this that was casual. At least, not for me.

"You with me, darlin'?" he asked, and I opened my eyes to find him watching me with those hellfire eyes, the hint of a smile still on his lips. "'Cause I'm about to lose it and I wanna take you with me when I go. Would love to make this last for you, V, but it's been a long fuckin' night." He was panting as he drove into me, and I could see the slight shake of his muscles as he held himself back.

"Yeah," I choked out. "I'm with you. Almost."

Couldn't make it too easy for him, could I?

"Then you better start askin' for it. Tell me what you want. What you need…"

I met his eyes again and said, "You know what I need."

At least, he used to.

His smile faded and with that, he fucked me, harder… harder, until I was sliding back along the love seat and my head was hanging off.

"Yeah… You feel so fuckin' tight, babe. So hot… Your tits are so… *fuck*," he said, squeezing my breasts until it almost hurt. So, yeah: he definitely remembered two things I needed… dirty talk and rough handling. "Can't believe I almost forgot how fuckin' fine these tits are."

Then he leaned down over me and shoved one breast up to meet his mouth, flicking and lapping his tongue over my nipple… until I groaned through my clenched teeth.

Oh, no. No, no, no.

None of this gentle tongue stuff.

"Harder," I told him, gasping for air.

He obliged, but it wasn't enough. Not enough to rid me of that feeling, his tongue flickering over my nipple, tasting me…

Then he did it again… licking, then sucking gently on me.

"*Harder*," I rasped. "You know I like it hard…"

"Yeah," he growled, slamming into me. "I remember."

"And don't fucking suck on my nipple like that."

"Like this?" He sucked my other nipple into his mouth and teased it with his tongue, lapping slowly, deliberately.

"Fuck… *Fuck off*, Jude… seriously."

He chuckled, but he didn't stop teasing my nipples, suckling, licking, kissing…

Then one of his hands slid up around my throat and grabbed me, squeezing just a little, holding me pinned as he pounded into me. I couldn't move, he had me pinned down so tight.

"*Harder*," I gasped as I fought for breath.

He let my nipple go with a pop.

"*Fuck*, V…"

He caught me up then, pulling me toward him, yanking me into his lap as he gave it to me. He held my hips down against him and fucked up into me, hard and deep. I wrapped myself around him, shuddering as he pummeled my clit, meaning to bury my face in his neck as I came, but he wouldn't let me. He nudged my face back with his and found my lips, kissing me, his strong tongue plundering my mouth.

I lost control, then.

Totally lost it…

I came, hard, as his tongue stroked mine, slippery wet and warm, as his mouth slid against mine, sucking… as he held my hips and fucked me in short, harsh strokes. I would've screamed bloody murder if his tongue wasn't filling my mouth, but as it was, I just moaned and rode him, frantically, and bit his tongue. Hard.

He growled into my mouth and a shudder tore through his body, seconds before his hips snapped up and he exploded into me.

Then he broke his mouth away, groaning.

I rode him slowly, drawing out the waves of his pleasure, kissing his face with my eyes closed and holding him tight… just savoring his ecstasy… riding it right along with him…

Until his body gradually relaxed and he hugged me, heaving a deep, satisfied sigh.

I opened my eyes.

His hooded gaze moved down my face and he smirked a little as he said, "That hard enough for you?"

"I could take it harder."

His eyes darkened and he kissed me, softly.

Then he lifted me and got up, setting me gently on the love seat. I watched him move toward his clothes—but I wasn't just gonna sit here while he got dressed and left. As rubbery as my legs were, as hard as my head was still spinning, even though most of my blood was nowhere near my brain... I got up, and started getting dressed first.

When I was fully dressed, I glanced over at him.

He was dressed too, watching me as he zipped up his hoodie. "You want me to walk you to your cabin?"

I looked away. "Nope. I'm good."

I felt him move toward me. He hooked a finger under my chin and lifted my face to meet his gaze. He searched my face, slowly, his dark eyes dead serious.

"You feelin' me, V?"

I scoffed. Then I lied to him.

I totally fucking lied.

"No," I said.

But *come on*...

Maybe Jude *was* an asshole. Fucking me like that—worse, *kissing* me like that—and then asking me if I was "feeling" him moments later?

I turned away, zipping up my jacket.

He caught my chin again and turned my face back to his.

"That's good." His dark eyes held mine in challenge, but his tone was gentle. "'Cause I told you long ago, you and me, darlin', we're not goin' down that road."

"And I told you," I said cooly, "that all roads lead to fucking. Which means this road is now closed."

He chuckled, his gaze dropping to my lips. "And what was that other thing you used to say..." His thumb brushed my cheek. "You never go back for seconds?"

I shrugged and pulled away, but I managed a small, coy smile. "First time for everything."

"Second time," he said, "the way I remember it."

"Yeah, well. I've never been great with math."

He laughed. Then he swatted my ass—like I was some fucking puppy he was sending on its way.

"Don't let the wild card thing bother you, V," he said. "You *are* wild. Nothing wrong with that."

Then he did the worst thing of all.

He grabbed my jacket so I couldn't leave, and leaned in and kissed me. I long, deep, passionate kiss that made my clit throb and my toes curl and my guts turn inside-out. It was the way a guy kissed you when he really, *really* liked you.

Except that Jude's affection for me only went so far.

Far enough to fuck me, apparently. But no further than that.

Well, *fuck him*.

I pulled away and walked away, without looking back. Letting him believe that was all I ever really wanted to be to him—the wild card; the party girl—and pretending I was okay with it.

But I wasn't okay.

I knew it as I pushed through the door and out into the crisp night air, and the cold reality of what just happened hit me, full force. Because it *wasn't* just a fuck.

And in the end, it had zero to do with revenge.

I *was* feeling Jude. A lot.

Just like I did back then.

A Dirty Deal

Author's Note

In *A Dirty Vow*, when Jesse and Katie head off to their luxury cabin to finally enjoy their wedding night alone, they don't go straight there. Instead, Jesse decides he needs to enjoy his new wife, *now*... And when they stop to go at it along the boardwalk in the woods, Jesse's ex-girlfriend, Elle, unfortunately—for her—sees them.

Later, in *A Dirty Lie*, we briefly glimpse Elle again, as she walks past a naked Roni, Dylan and Ash, outside Roni's cabin—just before Ash disappears into the night.

So, where is Elle headed in the dark all alone? And how is she doing? *Is* she having a nice night? Well... no. As Jesse so aptly puts it in *A Dirty Vow*, any fucking way you slice it, this wedding is not nice for Elle.

But fortunately for Elle, her night is about to take an unexpected turn...

Jaine

Chapter 1

Ash

Elle.

Long, platinum-blonde hair.

Unmistakable.

Wearing a puffy silver winter jacket and ripped jeans. Five-foot-seven, slim and tanned, with a tight ass, slender hands, steel-gray eyes, and a mouth I'd very possibly kill to kiss.

Dirty's bass player. My friend.

And the groom's ex-girlfriend.

Walking right past me, up the boardwalk.

I was standing there, naked and fucking frozen, cupping my goods in my hands, right next to Dylan. In front of Roni. The three of us were standing outside Roni's cabin, and she'd just informed us that we—Dylan and I—weren't stepping inside until we coughed up some condoms.

And now I was glad she did.

Because then Elle walked by.

And I forgot why I'd wanted into Roni's cabin in the first place.

What was Elle doing all alone? With a tote bag over one shoulder, wandering around in the dark, in the dead of night…

"Didn't see a thing," she said, a note of amusement in her voice, averting her eyes as she walked on by, waving us off. "Have a good one, boys and girl."

"*Damn*," Dylan muttered, his head already somewhere in Roni's bed, the rest of him shivering next to me. "I'll get the condoms." He kissed Roni on the cheek. Then my best friend and eternal wingman took off into the night.

I looked at Roni, and she looked at me.

We were alone. She was gorgeous. Sexy, curvy and willing. The guys didn't call her "wild card" for nothing. I'd heard the stories. Zane. Piper. Even Jude. They all had a story about Wild Card Roni.

And I could see why.

I'd kissed her last night at Katie's stagette party, danced with her, made out with her a bit.

But Elle wasn't at that party.

This was the first time Roni and I had ever been alone, and I really couldn't say what it would've felt like if we'd gotten to this moment without Elle walking by. Because the thing was, Elle *had* walked by.

And now *this* felt all wrong.

I raked my hand through my hair, bouncing on the balls of my feet, just fucking choking on it. Roni opened her mouth to say something, but I cut in first. "Me too." I took her hand and kissed it. I'd probably never kissed a woman's hand before. At least, not a woman who wasn't naked in my bed. Just seemed like the right thing to do now.

Because I couldn't remember ever getting this close to screwing a woman and blowing her off, either.

Then I took right off.

And fuck if I knew what I was doing.

All I knew was I had to get out of there.

I hightailed it up to my cabin and got dried off and dressed. Then I dug out some condoms and stuffed them into my leather jacket. Wasn't even sure why I did that.

All I was thinking about was Elle.

When she disappeared from the fire pit a while ago, I'd just assumed she went to bed. I'd tried to walk her to her cabin, but she wouldn't let me. Said she wanted to be alone.

But clearly she wasn't sleeping, and I didn't even know what to think about that. Except that it bothered me.

Bothered me enough that I couldn't fuck around with Roni, or even go to bed myself, while she was out there, alone.

On Jesse's wedding night.

Because that shit wasn't right.

When I headed back out into the night, the choice was easy: get laid, or go after Elle and make sure she's okay... as I approached Roni's cabin along the boardwalk, I just kept going. I went the way Elle had gone, down toward the fire pit, where the wedding after party had gone all night, with music and booze and skinny dipping.

But she wasn't there.

No one was there anymore, but at least some responsible soul —one of Dirty's management team, Brody or Maggie, no doubt— had put the fire out.

So I continued on... to the only other place the path delivered me: the hot springs down below, on the rim of the cove. As I wound my way down the rocky path, I saw her there.

Elle.

She was sitting in one of the little rock-lined pools, alone.

Her bag—and her clothes—were discarded on the rocks. Her back was to me; I could make out the curves of her slim shoulders in the moonlight.

Just as I opened my mouth to say something clever, hoping I

wouldn't scare the living shit out of her, she said, "Fuck off, Jude. I'm fine."

"Not Jude," I said, pausing on a rock above her.

She glanced up at me over her shoulder. "Oh. Hey, Ash."

Not exactly the warmest welcome a guy could hope for, but it would have to do. I knew this wasn't exactly a great night for her.

Who wanted to attend the wedding of an ex—an ex they were still in love with?

"Mind if I hop in?"

Even in the near-dark, I saw her eyebrows pinch together and her arms float protectively around herself.

"It's dark, Elle. I can't see shit."

It was true. Mostly because she was buried in water from the armpits down.

She sighed deeply and said, "Whatever." Then she sank back, resting her head against a rock she'd covered with a towel.

Good enough for me.

I ditched my jacket and boots, then stripped all the way down to my briefs—quickly. It was fucking frigid out, and I still hadn't warmed up after that skinny dip. I didn't see any panties on her pile of discarded clothes, but that was hardly conclusive evidence that she was naked in the water. Either way, I kept my underwear on, out of respect.

Naked or not, didn't seem like she was in the mood to deal with anyone's dick in her face. Even one as awesome as mine.

I got into the water and sank down next to her.

"*Shiiit…*" I sighed raggedly as the warmth hit me. Found a smooth spot to get comfortable against a rock and closed my eyes, letting the heat soak in and the cold melt away until I stopped shivering. Took a while.

Once I'd thawed out, I ventured, "Jude been up your ass tonight?"

"Yeah. He's prowling around here somewhere," she grumbled. "Checking up on me. The usual."

Yeah. I could understand how that might get annoying, given that Jude, while Dirty's head of security, was also Jesse's best friend.

I looked over at her. She was tense as fuck, her pretty face screwed up tight and shoulders up around her ears.

"I'm not even gonna ask how your night's going," I told her, "so you can relax."

Her shoulders dropped a little as she unclenched.

"How about you?" She eyed me sidelong. "Roni?"

"Not happening."

She cocked her head, assessing me. Maybe she was considering busting my balls a bit. Probably. I'd seen that unimpressed look on her face before. Many times, actually. Usually backstage or at some party while I was surrounded by willing groupies and she was on her way to somewhere else. "Dylan win the coin toss?" Her tone was all sarcasm, but the mood rolling off her was frigid with contempt.

"We don't coin toss for girls anymore," I informed her, unfazed. This girl could be a stone-cold bitch to me tonight and it wouldn't faze me. I knew her well enough to know what she was so pissed off about, and it had shit all to do with me.

Anyone who knew Elle would know why she was miserable today.

"Only did that when we were young and immature," I added.

"Uh-huh. So how do you decide who gets the first go?"

I smirked a little, considering how to word it. "We've learned to share."

"Hmm." Her tone was dismissive. Clearly she didn't want any more details on that. Usually she didn't want any details at all, so I wasn't sure why she was curious about this.

"I guess Roni's just not my flavor," I elaborated.

"Right. And what is your flavor these days?" Again, the contempt. Like it was my fault that Jesse Mayes, Dirty's lead guitarist and the man of her dreams, broke up with her like a year ago.

So maybe she was deep in a long-ass man-hating phase.

Still didn't faze me.

I just stared at her, admiring the way the moonlight kinda glowed off her long platinum hair, watching the strands float around her shoulders in the water. The way her face looked smooth and kinda silvery under the stars… and way too fucking young for such a bitter expression.

I wondered how long it'd been since she smiled, a giant, unstoppable smile. How long it'd been since she actually good and laughed.

Or got good and fucked… So good it made her toes curl, and she forgot about Jesse Mayes for a couple of fucking seconds.

"If you tell me yours," I said, deciding to go ahead and straight-up flirt with her, "I'll tell you mine."

What harm could flirting do?

We were undressed, in a hot pool under the stars, it was the middle of the night, and we were alone.

But Elle looked away, staring out over the waters of the cove, where the force of the ocean broke the waves against the rocks just below us.

Damn. I lost her there.

Of course, Elle and I rarely discussed sex or relationships. Not my choice. But she was incredibly careful about that. With me, even with her Dirty bandmates Dylan and Zane; basically all her male friends. Ever since the breakup with Jesse.

Actually, since things fell to shit between the two of them, she didn't talk to me about much at all. Not like she used to.

When she was crushing on Jesse, I couldn't shut her up about him. When it became more than a crush, I heard about that, too.

When she fell head-over-heels in love… I heard more than I could ever want to know about it.

Now? Not a fucking word about her feelings.

It was as if when she got dumped, she decided not to feel anything at all—other than to freeze up like an ice queen and loathe men.

"Alright," I offered, trying to keep things light, "I'll go first. I like shy, virginal girls who turn into nymphos once I get them in bed."

She scoffed under her breath. "That's a load of shit, Ash."

"Is it?" I challenged, deadpan. "I also like shy, virginal guys who turn into nymphos once I get them in bed."

"That's an even bigger load of shit."

"Why?"

She looked up to the sky and gave a small sigh. "Because I've seen the girls, and the guys, you hook up with." She was really starting to sound irritated. Though why my hook-up preferences would irritate her, I had no clue.

Other than occasionally checking me out when she thought I wasn't looking, Elle had never expressed an interest in hooking up with *me*.

But she was in a rough mood. She needed a punching bag, she could go ahead and take her frustrations out on me. I didn't mind.

"True fact…" I lounged back against the rocks, sinking deeper into the water. "I like churchgoers I can corrupt. The more virtuous, the better."

"Bullshit."

"I'm partial to nuns, actually."

She shook her head. "So full of it."

"Monks…"

She threw me one of her steely-eyed gazes. The kind that might send a lesser man running for the hills, tail between his legs.

"I'm serious."

"Don't try to play me, Ashley Player," she said. "You like bad girls and bad boys. The *badder* the better."

I shrugged. "Just because I hook up with them doesn't mean I like them."

For some reason, that seemed to rub her the wrong way. I could practically feel the night frosting over between us. Surprised the water didn't turn to ice. "You like the pretty party people, Ash. Admit it."

"Had a thing with a priest once," I mused, even as she made an annoyed huffing sound. "Actually, he was a priest-in-training, or something."

"You like Dylan."

Her words crackled in the night, like an assault weapon fired out of nowhere.

I did *not* see that coming.

She stared at me, and I stared at her.

Silence fell.

Actually, it slapped me in the face.

For a long, sharply painful moment, I couldn't breathe.

Not that *what* she'd said surprised me, exactly. I was just surprised she *would* say it. Because it really wasn't any of her business how I felt about Dylan. He was her drummer and her friend. But he was my *best* friend.

And it wasn't like I had a choice in how I felt about him.

When I found my voice again, I said, as cool as I could, "When are you gonna stop liking Jesse? That gonna happen anytime this goddamn century?"

She stood up with an abrupt splash. Water streamed off her body. And she must've been really pissed, because she was naked.

Like, completely naked.

No panties to be found.

Elle was famous. She was famous enough when I first met

her, as Dirty's bassist, but these days she was a veritable one-woman empire, with a solo music career on the side, a rising star in Hollywood, a charitable foundation, and a hot-as-shit makeup line—to list the highlights. Which meant she was incredibly fucking famous; way more famous than me.

She was also private as all hell about her personal shit.

Which meant you'd never find her flashing her goods on a "private" beach for the paparazzi or doing nude photos for Rolling Stone or "accidentally" leaking a sex tape to the media. She didn't skinny dip when the rest of us dropped our drawers and dove right in. She didn't go streaking through parties or humping randoms on the tour bus for everyone to see.

Which meant in the five years I'd known her, and our bands had toured together, I'd never seen her naked before.

I was seeing her now.

All lean and toned and sun-kissed and wet.

I saw her tits. Kinda medium-sized and that perfect tear-drop shape. Her nipples tight and flushed against the cold. The slim curves of her waist. The jewel in her navel ring glinting in the moonlight.

I saw her pussy. Neatly ladyscaped with just a delicate strip of blondish hair… right in my face.

I would've taken a closer look if I'd had the chance, but she was about to climb the fuck out of the pool, so I grabbed her arm and stopped her and looked her in the eye.

"I apologize," I said, sincerely. "Forget I said that. Now retract your claws and stay. It's not me you're really pissed at."

She stood there stubbornly for a long, tense minute as I stared into her eyes, willing myself not to gawk at the rest of her.

Then she softened and sank into the water, shrugging my hand off.

I let her go.

But my heart was beating, thudding, fast.

Elle settled back against a rock, an arm's length from me, and fell silent.

I could've reached out and touched her.

I didn't.

After a while, she said, "It's none of your fucking business, Ashley."

"I realize that."

"You're not in my band."

"Painfully aware of that."

Her eyes flashed to me and she softened some more, finally giving up on being pissed at me.

"You want a smoke?" I offered. I stood up to get one, because I couldn't sit still. A restless, frustrated energy was roiling inside me, making my guts twist.

And making my dick hard.

Lust. I was totally in lust with Elle. No matter how irritated she was with me, my dick didn't seem to care.

But this wasn't exactly a new discovery.

"No thanks," she said, not looking at me. "Just a beer, if you're getting out."

I hopped up out of the pool and grabbed a beer from her bag, popped it open and handed it to her, then fished a joint out of a cigarette case in my jacket, along with a lighter. I lit up and stood there a moment, just looking up at the moon, breathing in the pot smoke and the fucking freezing air, letting my lungs shudder and burn as my muscles jittered with cold.

Letting the discomfort of that other shit roll through me.

You like Dylan.

I took another drag, and as the weed gradually did its thing, I mellowed out.

I tucked the joint between my lips and got back in the water, setting the cigarette case, stocked with extra weed, on a nearby rock.

Elle glanced at me as I sank back beside her. "For the record," she said quietly, "and just so we're clear, and you never have to ask me again, I will always like Jesse."

"Fair enough."

"But," she added, "I don't love him anymore."

Right.

"Well, I'll always like Dylan." It came out before I was sure I should commit to saying it out loud, but here with Elle, what the fuck did it matter? I'd probably tell her anything she wanted to know, if she asked. And not like this was new information, either. "You say anything to him, though, and I'll have to kill you. You know that, right?"

"You think he doesn't know?" she said simply.

I didn't answer that.

"He's not stupid, Ash."

"Don't wanna talk about it, Elle."

I didn't. Admitting it to her was one thing. Didn't mean I wanted to have an open forum discussion. I didn't really give a shit what Elle or anyone else thought about it.

She went silent. And I could tell she was feeling a little sorry for bringing it up. She never had before, though obviously she'd figured it out.

Maybe the whole fucking world had figured it out by now.

I really didn't give one fuck.

As long as it didn't weird Dylan out and mess things up with the best friend I'd ever had.

"You know I'd never say anything," Elle said with a small sigh. "You've always been cool about my bullshit with Jesse." She looked at me. "Everyone else gets all tense and tiptoes around it. Even Dylan. Zane. 'How you doing, hon?' They talk to me like I'm some car crash victim recovering, too slowly, in the hospital. Like they can only approach me during scheduled visiting hours and speak in hushed tones. Like they're just waiting for someone to magically appear and give them an update on my prognosis."

"Things are looking up," I said, turning on my best charlatan doctor voice. "She really came through that last bout of screaming diarrhea. She's a real trooper."

Her lips quirked in a slight smile. The first one I'd seen all night. "See? That's what I mean. It doesn't scare you."

"What doesn't?"

She got quiet, for a long moment. Then she said, "My broken heart."

I stared at her, just trying to come to terms with that. With how totally fucking wrong she was.

"It scares the shit out of me, Elle," I told her. "That's why I make jokes."

And for some reason, that made her smile.

"When did you become such a good friend to me?" she mused, sipping her beer. It sounded like an accusation.

"Who knows." I took a drag off my joint. "You're tight with Dylan. I'm tight with Dylan. Guess it was just part of the deal."

"Uh-huh." She narrowed her eyes at me. "You're very sneaky about it, you know? One minute, I'm walking into my dressing room backstage to find you screwing a bunch of groupies on my makeup table… Disgusting, by the way."

I just shrugged, as if to say *All in a day's work*.

"And the next… you're baking a five-layer cake for my birthday."

"Guilty as charged."

She was skewering me with her cool grey eyes, but she didn't have me fooled. Elle could act like an ice queen all she wanted, but I knew she was all warm, soft pussycat inside.

You just had to figure out how to rub her the right way.

"You are one confusing specimen, Ashley Player."

"Ah, but I'm never boring."

"I'll give you that. You're about the farthest thing from boring I can imagine."

I took that as a compliment.

"Just following my mom's advice," I said, using that same humor I used to deflect everything that had ever come close to hurting me. "'Whatever you do, never bore the ladies.'"

Elle half-smiled, but seemed to catch herself before she committed to anything like laughing. "I call bullshit. Your mom never said that."

"She did. Right before she left." I took a drag off my joint and looked her in the eye. "As it turns out, the bored ladies leave."

Chapter 2

Elle

W ell, shit.

Ash had never told me that before; that his mom had left him. I didn't exactly know that. Just knew she wasn't in his life.

He'd never really been the kind of friend who talked about that kind of thing. Like a lot of men I'd known, he tended to shy away from emotional stuff. Or made jokes about it.

At least, his own emotional stuff.

My stuff… a different story. Ash minced no words when it came to my shit. And as it turned out, that was just the kind of friend I'd needed this past year.

Someone who could look me in the eye and treat me like a normal, whole person instead of some broken disaster victim.

Someone fun, who made me smile when I couldn't even remember how.

Somehow who kept the party rolling. Who kept life rolling.

Who took it upon himself to bake me a five-layer chocolate birthday cake with custard in the middle and cherries on top. Not because I was a huge fan of chocolate cake, but because he knew I'd appreciate the surprise party he threw me along with it, with just a few of the most important people in my life in attendance, and that they—my friends and family—*would* like the cake. That it would make them happy, which meant making me happy, at a time when I'd almost forgotten *how* to be happy. When I was so caught up in other things that I'd almost forgotten it even was my birthday.

That kind of friend.

But it was somewhere around that party that I started to get the feeling Ash liked me as something more than a friend. Which was to say that it became apparent he wanted to fuck me.

Very soon after I met him, Ashley, the legendary Player, went and got himself a girlfriend. My friend Summer, actually. She wasn't my friend then. I didn't know her. But when my band met his at a festival, over five years ago, and Dylan and Ash became fast friends, Ash's band, the Penny Pushers, quickly became a staple on our tours. I met Summer through Ash, and she and I had become great friends over the years.

Somewhere along the way, Ash and Summer broke up. He went on playing. I drifted in and out of a few relationships.

Then I was with Jesse.

Then Jesse broke up with me.

And Ash threw me an amazing birthday party.

And I started to get that feeling when he looked at me. Especially when we were alone.

The feeling I was getting right now.

"When did your mom leave?" I asked, carefully, half-expecting him to blow it off with a joke.

But he just gazed off into the night as he smoked his joint and seemed to be thinking about it. "I was thirteen. She was never mother of the year, even when she was around," he added lightly.

"So don't feel too bad about it. I have an aunt who kicks ass, so it all balances out."

"Aunt Ginny," I said. "I remember her. The one in Montana?"

"Colorado."

"Right."

A silence fell, not uncomfortable, though I could still feel that look he was giving me, even when I wasn't looking back at him. *Especially* when I wasn't looking.

No way I could ignore that smoldering interest, burning into me.

Ash was all smoldering heat and angsty intensity, and even though I knew his lighter side—his ridiculous side, the one Dylan brought out in him more than anyone—I could imagine the kind of flaming beast he'd be in bed. All lean and cut and tattooed...

Not that I'd ever really allowed myself to dwell on those thoughts.

It was too... strange. He was a friend. So many of our friends were friends that he felt, weirdly, like family.

Though Jesse felt like family too, and I'd still fallen for him.

Ash, though... he just wasn't my type.

Except that he kind of was.

I stole a glance at him. Inky black hair, gorgeous face. High cheekbones, straight nose, all chiseled, fascinating angles, the kind a girl could get lost in. Dark eyebrows drawn together over blue, blue eyes. Tattoos visible on his shoulders, and a surfer's bod—though most of that was hidden beneath the water right now.

Not like I hadn't taken a good, long look—or a hundred—before. It was pretty epic, as far as male bodies went.

Ashley Player was a thing of beauty.

So maybe I just wasn't exactly sure why I hadn't jumped his bones yet? Or let him jump mine...

Other than the fact that it had never felt quite right to me.

Or maybe it was because he didn't exactly get his last name, his stage name—*Player*—solely because he played guitar.

Or maybe, just maybe, it was because some small part of me was measuring him against Jesse Mayes... and no living human male had yet risen to that bar in my mind.

Right. That bullshit.

"You remember that time in Colorado?" he asked, kind of dreamily, which meant the pot was probably going to his head. "In the hot tub." His slightly-hooded eyes roamed over my face as he spoke. "You were all steamed up, like you are now, in that hot silver bikini of yours..." He roamed off there, and I got a little uncomfortable imagining where his mind was at. "You were so fucking drunk," he went on, "and happy, and that preppy douche tried to pick you up? Had no idea who you were. He was all fascinated with your platinum hair and your belly button piercing. Like you were some kind of exotic creature out of his wet dreams he couldn't actually believe was real."

"If I recall," I said dryly, "you got me drunk." I remembered that night alright, too clearly. Ash and his bright ideas. The man could bartend with the best of them, and decided to make homemade Bailey's Irish Cream. It tasted so good I made the mistake of drinking about a blender full of it myself. I was epically sick the next day. "I can't remember ever feeling that gross."

"You were a hot mess," he agreed. "You got lost looking for ice, and ended up in my hotel room in the middle of the night."

"I remember."

"I would've kept you there, tucked you in and kept you, if Jesse hadn't come to collect you." He stared at me with that smoldering, one-hundred-degree Fahrenheit look of his. "You know that, right?"

Yeah, I kinda knew.

I also knew he was flirting with me, and it wasn't the harmless kind of flirting friends sometimes did, that didn't really mean a thing.

There was heat behind it.

And a not-so-subtle challenge.

Actually, he was being downright cocky. Which meant he was being his usual Ashley Player self, but for some reason, it was more flattering than usual. More welcome.

Usually I just let Ash's attempts to flirt with me roll off. He threw it out there, I ignored it.

This time, I smiled. Admittedly, Ash seemed to care a lot about making me smile.

Too much, maybe.

But right now, I'd take it. Because when had it become okay for me to go through life without smiling?

Smiling was something I used to do easily, and regularly. Why wouldn't I? I had an amazing life. I had the band, my career. I had the music. Unlike a lot of other rock stars I knew, I had a solid family, too. Two loving parents, and I grew up with money. I never really wanted for anything, including love.

But then there was Jesse.

And everyone on Earth knew how that turned out.

I took a swig of my beer and just tried to feel grateful, for everything I had. I tried to feel, really *feel*, deep down, happy for Jesse and the love he'd found.

But just like every other time I'd tried to do that since we broke up, and he met Katie… I just couldn't.

I felt the tears sparking in my eyes before I could stop them.

And Ash said, "It's okay to still be pissed. And hurt. And totally fucking sad. Or whatever the fuck you feel, Elle. Maybe no one's told you that. But it's okay."

"Summer's told me," I said. "And Jessa, and Maggie. And now you. But I think everyone else is just waiting to exhale when

I stop feeling what I'm feeling, so we can all go back to life as usual."

"Well, fuck them," he said. "There is no 'life as usual.' Life is whatever the fuck it is, right now. And if it's you with a broken heart sitting here with me drinking beer on Jesse's wedding night while he fucks his bride in their cabin, so fucking be it."

Yeah. Never one to mince words.

But I kinda loved that about Ash. The truth was, I was surrounded by yes men, and yes women, all fucking day. I preferred it when people gave it to me straight. Never more so than after Jesse broke up with me—and told me he hadn't really been happy with me all along.

Because who needed that?

I never wanted to be in that situation again. Thinking things were something that they totally weren't.

"Alright," I said, and I raised my beer, sniffing back the half-formed tears. "Here's to me and my broken heart. And to Jesse and his bride."

Ash raised what was left of his joint and tapped it to the neck of my beer bottle. I took a swig and he took a drag.

"Her name's Katie," he said, in the silence that followed.

"Uh-huh."

How could I forget? Her name was as cute as the rest of her. And now her name was Katie *Mayes*. So there was really no getting away from it.

"If you use her name, it humanizes her, and makes it harder to hate her."

"Thanks for the tip."

"You need any others," he offered, "I've got a few."

"I'll keep it in mind."

He was still watching me. Actually, I didn't think he'd taken his eyes off me more than once or twice since he joined me in the pool.

And right now, it was more than flattering.

But it still wasn't enough.

"Do you think I'll ever have that?" I asked him quietly, as if anyone could hear us. "You know, what they have. The way they looked up there at the altar…"

Ash seemed to consider that. "Do you think I will?" he countered.

"I don't know. Do you want that?"

He shrugged and kind of smiled at me. That killer, *I'm a crazy-hot-lead-singer-without-a-care-in-the-world* smile. "I don't know."

I nodded, like I understood that. But really, I didn't. Then I confessed, "I do."

"Then you will."

He was probably right about that. I knew he was.

Right now, though, I just couldn't feel it.

"Look," he said, "I don't know about any of this standing-up-at-the-altar shit, Elle. Weddings aren't exactly my thing. But I do know a thing or two about women and men in bed."

"You don't say."

"And I'd take you to bed over Katie in a hot minute, any day of the week."

I didn't want to be flattered by that, but… "She's not your flavor?"

"Not even close."

"You're saying that because she's with Jesse and she's unavailable anyway."

"I'm saying that because it's true."

Maybe. But even if he meant it, he was just flirting. I knew that. And just like every other time he'd done it, I knew I couldn't take it seriously.

I couldn't take *him* seriously.

I didn't want more with Ash than friendship. One tall, dark

and complicated rock star was enough for me. *No more guitar players*; I'd promised myself that after the breakup with Jesse.

And Ash wasn't only a lead guitarist. He was a lead singer, which was worse.

Double the ego.

Double the drama.

Not what I needed in my life.

What I needed, probably, was an accountant. Someone logical and dependable and predictable, with not one tattoo, who couldn't play a musical instrument to save his life, who'd never been on tour, never stepped onstage, never had swarms of groupies begging to fuck him—and fucking with his head.

A normal guy, with a normal life.

Yeah. That was probably where my love life was headed, if I had any sense at all.

But a little flirting along the way… It felt good. I could admit that to myself. Ash was scorching hot, and yes, he'd had more than his share of women, but right now, he was all about me. Maybe it was only for a few minutes in the middle of the night when no one else was around to compete for his attention, but I'd take his compliments.

"Thank you for saying that. It shouldn't feel good, but it does."

"It's meant to feel good," he said, still watching me. Still flirting.

"Yeah," I said, sipping my beer. "I guess I just haven't heard enough of that kind of thing lately."

He laughed. His teeth were white against his skin in the moonlight, and his face lit up. His eyes crinkled at the corners. And, damn…

Ash just sitting around, looking all restless and angsty? Gorgeous.

But Ash laughing? Devastating.

"Shiiit," he teased. "You're shitting me, right?"

Wish I was. "Nope."

"Not possible. You're Elle Goddamn Delacroix. As if you don't hear it everyday. People telling you how hot you are?"

"It's different, though." I shrugged. "Different coming from a man. You know, a man…" I trailed off, not sure how to finish that. Not sure I wanted to.

"A man who wants to fuck you," he finished for me. Our eyes locked. "You must hear it from those on a daily basis too."

I wish.

"You'd be surprised," I confessed. "I don't exactly let men get close lately. You know, I could go entire days talking to no one at all. Have Joanie take my calls. Hole up somewhere and shut everyone out. It's kind of… pathetic."

It was true. And I'd done it, often enough; had my assistant screen the shit out of my personal calls, emails, everything.

"Really," he said, like he didn't believe me. "So it's true, then. The hottest girls sit at home alone on Friday night?"

"What can I say. You'd be surprised how lonely it is at the top." I said it casually, like it wasn't a big thing. But in reality, it was the *biggest* thing.

I knew I still had my band, my career, my family and my friends. I'd probably always have them. I still had Jesse, even, as a bandmate.

But I'd never felt more lonely, more *alone*, than when he broke up with me.

"Wouldn't surprise me at all," Ash said.

He fished out a fresh joint and lit up. He offered it to me, but I waved it away. I didn't feel like smoking up. The booze I'd drank tonight was bad enough; I was afraid, with this wedding, I was hovering on the edge of some kind of deep, ugly, bottomless depression, and drugs were hardly gonna help.

Ash took a drag, eying me.

"Joanie always puts my calls through," he said after a moment.

"Yeah," I admitted. "She does."

"And why is that?"

"Because…" I stopped there. *Because I like talking to you,* didn't seem like the right thing to say. Sounded too much like flirting back—or giving him the green light to feel me up. "Because you're my friend."

"So is Zane," he challenged. "Willing to bet you've screened his ass plenty of times."

"Maybe," I admitted. "A time or two, over the years."

"How about Jesse?" he asked. "You take all his calls these days?"

"Most of them," I mumbled into my beer.

"Uh-huh. So how come you take mine?"

"Because… You never make me feel bad about myself for being so… fucking broken."

Because talking to you always makes me feel better.

That was the whole truth of it, but I didn't say that either.

"How about now?" he pressed. "You sorry you let me in here with you?"

"There's hardly a door on the hot springs," I said dryly. "Couldn't exactly keep you out."

"Sure you could. You want me to leave, you just say the word."

I didn't say a thing.

And the water seemed to heat up several more degrees off the look he gave me.

Wow…

I wasn't even sure what to think about my male friend's sex eyes hitting me so hard between the legs.

But I definitely wasn't ignoring them like I usually did.

"So how is it that no man's told you he wants to fuck you lately?" he asked.

I considered that. Considered how far I wanted to take that answer. But I was starting to feel a little daring here. Enjoying Ash's flirting just a little too much. Because it was making me feel something I hadn't felt in a really long time. Hadn't allowed myself to feel, maybe, since Jesse rejected me.

Desired.

"I don't know. Maybe they did and I just wasn't listening."

"That sounds a hell of a lot more likely," he said.

Then I decided to make a bold confession, that was definitely in the realm of TMI. "I haven't been with anyone since Jesse."

Ash stared at me. The joint stopped partway to his mouth. "No one?"

"Nope."

"But… you guys broke up in, like, March."

"April," I said.

Which meant it had been exactly nine months since I'd gotten any.

Well, actually… it had been about ten months. Because those last few weeks between Jesse and I were not good. And he'd barely touched me.

I cringed at that awful memory. The way I did every time I remembered how rough things had become between us toward the end. How quickly I went from feeling over the moon to terrified he was going to leave me.

I'd never feared losing anyone or anything so much. And I'd never been more bereaved over a loss. It was like trying to get over a death; it was that painful. And that near-impossible.

Ash was still looking at me, and suddenly I felt uncomfortable exposing my total lack of sex life to him—a male rock star. A gorgeous, sexually promiscuous rock star.

In other words, a guy who probably got laid within minutes, if not seconds, of any old time he felt like it.

"What about all the guys I see you with?" he asked. "All the fucking time. You've got, like, a dude harem swarming around you wherever you go."

"Right. They're called security guys. And roadies. And publicists, and personal trainers, and massage therapists—"

"And horny fans," he concluded, clearly not buying my excuses.

I shrugged that off. "I don't know. Guess I just never close the deal." I sipped my beer, washing down the truth of it. "I blow them off, or I get Jude or someone to do it for me."

"Huh." He seemed to be digesting that, gradually. "Well, you know you could remedy that anytime you want, right? At least you have options."

"Maybe I don't want options," I said, and the truth of it was painful.

Embarrassing.

Because even though I knew I shouldn't, even though it was fucking bullshit and it was painful and masochistic and *he* was totally fucking taken by someone else, there was a part of me that was still hanging on. A really fucking stupid part of me, that hadn't gotten the message yet. That just couldn't fucking process the fact that my chance with Jesse Mayes had passed, and that he would never again be mine.

That he never really was mine.

Because he never loved me that way.

The way I loved him.

"So…" Ash said. "You don't love him anymore, but you still want him. Is that it?"

He waited, staring at me, until I could bring myself to answer that.

"Does that make me pathetic?" I asked, my voice small in the night, as I surrendered to the fact. "Please just tell me I'm fucking pathetic. Maybe it will help me to snap out of it, once and for all."

"No, Elle," he said, his voice low and unusually serious. Actually, it was filled with compassion, and roughened by just the slightest edge of envy. "It makes you human."

Chapter 3

Ash

Yeah. She wanted him.

And if she was still this hung up on Jesse, after all this time, and after just watching him *marry* someone else, she obviously hadn't gotten whatever closure she needed out of that situation.

All you had to do was take one look at Jesse with Katie to know Elle wasn't getting one last romp with him, for old time's sake, to get him out of her system. So no closure was coming there. And if she still wasn't fucking anyone else, there had to be something holding her back from getting on with her fucking life. Because this girl could get laid in a hot minute.

For example: right here. Right now.

Any-fucking-where she wanted.

I knew female musicians on the road—even married ones—who had a steady stream of fanboys snuck up to their hotel rooms and out the back door again by their staff. Men weren't the only ones who played those games. And Elle had the power—and the looks—to do it. She could've had them lined up around the block if that was what she wanted.

But clearly, she didn't want that at all.

"You never had the breakup party, did you?" I ventured, already knowing the answer.

She cocked an eyebrow at me. "Breakup party?"

"Whenever you have a breakup, you've gotta have a party. Like an epic party. The worse the loss, the bigger the party's gotta be, to balance everything out."

Which meant Elle needed one hell of an epic breakup party.

She smiled at me, slowly, so maybe we were getting somewhere. "That's kinda ridiculous, Ash."

I shrugged. "Works. Every time. When I broke up with Summer, had the biggest breakup party ever, at Zane's place in L.A.. Woke up at some ski lodge in Alaska, I shit you not, with this hot Iranian-American couple who ran a traveling freak show. Think I picked them up at the airport. Had a new tattoo. Hangover lasted three days." I grinned at the memory. "Best breakup ever."

"I heard about that," she said, not nearly as impressed as I was with that little tale. "The Alaska part, anyway. You know Zane put you on that plane, right?"

I shrugged. "I would've done the same to him."

It was true; Elle's lead singer and I had spent the better part of the last five years in an ongoing swinging dick contest. Clash of the lead singers. He won, most of the time, since he had the bigger band and the bigger bank. Bigger everything—dick included.

But the fact was, the dude made me laugh. He rivaled my antics with women. He had a voice I'd never admit I envied like I did. If I wasn't lead singer of my own band, I'd definitely want to be in his. I could never get in bed with his inflated ego, but other than that, Zane Traynor was a hard guy to find fault with.

Unless, maybe, if you were a chick.

"Hmm," Elle said, with a tone that said *Fucking men.* "And what's the tattoo?"

"That's the part that concerns you about that story, babe?"

She leaned over and poked me in the shoulder. "You're not gonna show it to me?"

"Undercarriage. Trust me, you don't wanna see it."

She leaned back and stared at me. "Undercarriage...?"

"It's under my balls, way up my thigh." When she just kept staring at me, her slim eyebrows rising higher on her forehead, I sighed and elaborated, "It's a prissy fucking pink flower that says *Danny 4Ever.*"

She smashed her lips together, maybe stifling a laugh. "Who's Danny?"

"No idea."

At that, she burst out laughing.

Fucking *finally.*

I'd searched my memory banks, and I was pretty fucking sure it'd been about a goddamn year since I'd heard the girl laugh— like *really* fucking laugh.

"You've got a tattoo between your legs that says *Danny 4Ever*, and you don't know who Danny is?"

"Yup."

She was silent a moment as she sipped her beer. Then she said, "You must have some idea. Like is Danny a girl? Or a guy?"

"No clue."

"Wow, Ash."

"I know, right?"

"I don't think you do know."

I narrowed my eyes at her through the smoke of my joint. "I know you think I'm a loose cannon."

"Not a loose cannon. More of a... free spirit, dancing to the beat of your own drum." Her smile faltered, then vanished. "You know... the kind that's always breaking shit along the way." As she looked at me, my heart sped up a little, doing this weird, heavy throb in my chest. Because there was something in her tone…

Like she *cared* that I was always breaking shit?

"And why do you say that?"

"Because," she said, still serious. "You don't remember who Danny is. But I'd bet you anything at all that he or she remembers *you.*"

I didn't know how to take that.

I just stared at her in the dark, the steam off the water and the smoke from my joint softening my vision. Then I looked up at the stars.

Let her words sink into me.

It was either the most romantically flattering thing anyone had ever said to me… or it was just plain sad.

Maybe it was both?

"Point taken," I murmured, and I took another drag.

"Do you have any idea at all?" she asked me. "I mean… you could be someone's Jesse Mayes."

"Huh?" I blinked at her. "The fuck does that mean?"

I liked Jesse well enough. He and I would never be best bros; we just didn't have that kind of chemistry. But we were cool.

Didn't mean I wanted to be compared to him in the relationship department. Not in Elle's mind.

"It means, do you even know how many hearts you've broken?"

"Do you?" I countered.

She didn't answer that. She didn't seem to like the thought of it, but no fucking way Elle Delacroix, platinum princess, hadn't broken a heart or two over the years. Or a hundred.

"All this talk of broken hearts is getting me down," I told her, taking another hit off my joint. Between the hot water and the weed and Elle, I was relaxed, buzzing, and decently content. But I was also hard as fuck, my cock throbbing to the point of distraction. "Let's turn this night the fuck around already."

"And how would we do that?"

"We could fuck," I said bluntly.

"Excuse me?"

As if she hadn't heard me.

"However you want," I told her, and maybe it was the pot loosening my tongue, but I fucking meant it. "Right now. Or whenever you want. It doesn't even have to mean anything. It can if you want it to. Or it can just be a friends thing."

She shook her head, looking kinda stunned, but she shouldn't have been. She knew I was hard up for her, right? "A 'friends' thing?"

"You know. Friends with benefits."

Even as I said it, I knew I was hoping for more. That I wanted more.

If I could get it.

But with her, I'd probably take *anything* I could get.

It's not that I was in love with Elle. She hadn't let me get close enough to fall in love with her. Yes, we were friends. But I'd never really gotten behind the veil she wore to shroud herself from the rest of the world. With me, she was Elle, the musician. The famous girl. The rock star. She'd never let me get near the real Elle—the girl inside all that other shit.

Every time I so much as tried to look at her that way, really look at her, really *see* her, she got conveniently scarce.

But the thing was, I knew I could probably fall for her if she let me.

Maybe that's what she was so afraid of.

I could just as easily enjoy the sex and walk away, if she really wanted me to.

Maybe.

Hard to know for sure when we hadn't even gone there yet.

"You want to get over Jesse, right?" I said. "So use me to get over him."

She was silent, so I went on.

"You can use my body. I don't mind being used. Whatever you like, I'm game."

She was staring at me, guarded, but she'd gone really still. Not-breathing still. And not just because she was scared.

Because she was thinking about my offer. I knew it when she drew a shuddery breath.

"That's a bad idea, Ash," she said softly.

"Is it?"

"Yes."

"You sure about that?"

"Yes," she said, her tone hardening.

"But how do you know unless you try?"

"It's a bad, *bad* idea, Ashley," she said emphatically.

"Or maybe it's not."

"It *is*," she insisted. "Completely. Actually, in the history of bad ideas, that may go down as the *most*—"

"Alright, alright." I raised my hands in mock surrender and blew it off. "You win. I was fucking kidding anyway."

But we both knew I wasn't.

"Right…"

"Serious. You're too skinny and too blonde for me," I told her. "And too gorgeous." I smashed out my roach on a rock and tossed it into the bush. Then I looked her in the eyes, my face carefully blank. "Who likes skinny blondes anyway?"

"Uh-huh," she said, sipping her beer. "We are really going out of style."

"Exactly. You probably couldn't get my dick up if you tried."

At that, her eyes flared. But I couldn't really read them in the dark. Had no idea if she thought that was hilarious, ridiculous, or insulting. Or if she knew it was a lie.

If she had any idea how hard I already was, just flirting with her.

She swallowed her beer and said, with a bit of bite, "That's good. Because I wouldn't want your dick up. You're way too tall, dark and egotistical for me, Ash."

But we both knew that wasn't true, either.

Chapter 4

Elle

"A m I?" he said, and he gave me such a smoldering, *Let's fuck right now* look, my pussy clenched in response.

It had been a long, long time since a man looked at me like that.

Or since I *noticed* a man looking at me like that.

But what the hell was I saying? My words were loaded with flirtation. With *challenge*. And you didn't challenge a guy like Ashley Player to fuck you.

Unless you wanted to get fucked.

He knew as well as I did that "tall, dark and egotistical" was kind of my happy place. Despite my best intentions, it was totally my happy place. Exhibit A, Jesse Mayes.

Fuck accountants.

I might as well have just spread my legs and told him to put it in.

This was the first time I'd full-on flirted back with Ash, ever, but I wasn't really prepared for the result of that flirting: his hand, slipping onto my thigh under the water as his blue-eyed gaze darkened and he ran his pierced tongue over his lip.

"I'm sorry," I blurted, "I don't know what I'm saying. I'm just kind of depressed tonight. Or something…"

His hand froze, mid-thigh.

Then he withdrew the hand and I just sat looking at him, feeling like an ass, trying to figure out what to say that didn't make me sound like a total bitch. A messed-up bitch who was so tired of apologizing for her shitty moods.

"I shouldn't have said that, Ash."

"It's okay," he said lightly.

"It's not. I mean, you are tall, dark, and…" I trailed off. "I shouldn't be flirting with you. I'm not trying to lead you on."

"Okay."

"It's just been a rough night."

"I know."

"Are we good?"

"We're good," he said. "We'll always be good."

But I wasn't so sure.

Silence fell between us. Silence filled with the sounds of the night, the rushing water of the cove lapping against the rocks and peeling away again, the babbling of the hot springs, the occasional chirp of an animal or insect in the woods. The sky was lightening over the trees; the sun would be coming up soon. And it seemed so grossly wrong, so unfair, that this day, the first day after Jesse's wedding, would start off with my heart still such a mess.

But I did not know what to say, or do, to make it better.

"You know what we need?" I looked over to find Ash watching me. "Music," he answered himself.

Then he stood up, water sluicing off his surfer's body—his lean, toned body. His sun-darkened skin… the tattoos that ran down both arms and across one pec, down the side of his torso, and down one hip, disappearing into his underwear. My gaze dropped to his package, clearly defined as the wet black fabric clung to him like a second skin.

I almost choked on my intake of breath.

He was *hard*.

And it was beyond obscene.

He might as well have been naked. I could see *everything*. Even the outline of the smooth, hard stud where he was pierced, at the head of his—

I dropped my gaze, which now landed on the inside of his thigh. Maybe I was hoping for a glimpse of that flower tattoo that said *Danny 4Ever*…

No luck.

It must've been really high up there. His briefs were definitely… brief.

I sipped my now-warm beer and averted my gaze as he climbed out of the water. It was really no big deal. I'd seen Ash's dick before. Not on purpose, but sometimes parties got wild, guys got drunk, and wearing clothes became low on their priority list.

But I'd never actually looked at it *that* way.

Mostly because even when I'd seen it, it had been hot on the tail of someone else. Namely Summer, or any number of people he'd hooked up with since they broke up.

But I was definitely looking at it—at *him*—that way now, as he bent over to dig something from inside his leather jacket and his sculpted bod shone all wet and sleek and hard in the moonlight. He fiddled around with his phone a bit, and I felt kinda guilty gawking.

I tore my eyes away again and took another sip of warm beer, my heart beating faster than it should in my chest.

He came back to the water holding a small, portable speaker in the palm of one hand. He flicked it on, and some kind of sexy dance song filled the air. I didn't know the song, but I recognized the style of the DJ and the voice; it was Calvin Harris.

Yeah. Sexy…

He set the speaker on a rock and used his sweater to dry himself off a bit as he shivered. His cock was still in my line of sight, though it was looking a little less-enthused in the frigid night air. He started to put his clothes on.

And I felt kinda… disappointed.

Fully dressed, he reached for my hand. "Come on," he said.

When I hesitated, he rolled his eyes and turned his head away.

"I won't look. Just do it fast or you're gonna freeze."

"I'm gonna freeze regardless. I was kinda hoping to stay in here until the sun at least came up."

"Still gonna freeze," he said. "That's why we're gonna dance."

Just then, the beat of the song kicked in. Ash looked down at me out of the corner of his eye and smirked.

"Welcome to your breakup party."

Okay. That got me.

I had to smile back. I totally grinned, actually.

"Always wanted one of those," I said.

I took his hand and let him haul me up out of the water. He was polite enough to make a show of looking away, though when I slipped on the rocks and bumped up against him, naked, his jaw clenched. Then I got dressed, as fast as I could, shivering all the way. I didn't look at him as I did it, so for all I knew he was helping himself to the show. But honestly, I was too cold to care.

I used the towel I'd brought to dry off, hastily, but I was still so damp that my tight jeans stuck to me and I couldn't get them all the way up over my hips to zip them. I didn't care about that either. I'd barely gotten everything on and my jacket zipped up when Ash grabbed me—and started spinning me around.

"Come on, you're gonna freeze," he urged.

"Already frozen," I complained.

But I went with it.

Mostly because Ash was a good dancer. He had a serious musician's rhythm and an athlete's body. He danced like a rock guy, which meant more jumping up and down than anything, but that worked for me. It worked for the song. It had a great, heavy, driving beat. Within seconds we had a two-person dance party going.

It felt good. Kinda freeing.

Tension-relieving.

Who needed sex?

My best guess of the song title was, "You Used To Hold Me." At least that's what I gathered from the repeated chorus line. As I moshed around in the near-dark with Ash, he sung along to it, kinda serenading me, and kept grabbing my hips to twirl me around... and I felt fucking giddy.

Before I knew it I was skipping around like an idiot.

I was fucking *giggling*.

Had I drank that much tonight?

I loved to dance, and I loved dance music. Summer—also known as DJ Summer—had worked on my solo album with me; it was mostly electronic rock with a few straight-up dance songs. Which was probably why Ash was playing this for me. He'd never struck me as much of a dance music lover.

But why the hell was I skipping and giggling in the woods in the middle of the night, with Ash?

He kept serenading me, with increasingly dramatic emphasis, like some super-hot Broadway actor, swinging me around... then dipping me low over his arm.

And I felt a rush of... something.

When he pulled me back up, plastering me—on purpose—against his chest, I told him, "You're an idiot." But I was grinning like a fool.

I couldn't remember when I'd felt this relaxed or this good about anything.

It had been that long.

Too long.

"I know," he said.

Then he kissed me.

Actually, he smashed, mouth-first, against me. And I saw it coming. It wasn't like I didn't know the instant it was about to happen. The darkening of his eyes, the lowering of his eyelids, the fading of his smile right before he did it.

But I let him do it.

I let him smear his lips over mine, hot and wet and tasting of sweet-smoky pot. I let him shove me open and slide his tongue, hot and strong, against mine.

I felt the smooth ball of his tongue piercing, and as it ran over my tongue, heat tore down my spine.

Then he started walking me up the rocky path toward the boardwalk.

And I let him.

He wrapped his arms around me, his hands wandering all over me, and he made out with me like he'd wanted this for a very long time.

And it was totally getting me hot…

Any fear I'd ever had about whether or not it would be worth crossing the line with Ash was allayed. Because no question, the man knew exactly what to do with his tongue.

I could only imagine he knew what to do with the rest of him.

And I'd seen the size of his hard-on.

Oh, yeah… This was happening.

When we reached the boardwalk, he pulled away, breathing deeply in the dark, his smoldering gaze locked on me. "You gonna let me fuck you?" he said, his voice rough with lust. "Or should I stop now?"

"Don't stop," I said, pulling him to me by his jacket. "Well... unless you don't have a condom?"

"I have a condom," he murmured, then he kissed me again, thoroughly. He kissed my face. He kissed my neck, sucking and licking, dragging the ball of his stud up my throat.

And I just let him, savoring the feeling of being kissed.

"How do you want it? Back up at my cabin, in front of the fire...?" He was kissing his way down my chest, unzipping my jacket as he went, fumbling with my sweater. "On the fucking floor...?" He was walking me backwards now, along the board-walk, as he kissed and pawed at me.

And I felt fucking high off of all of it.

It was that reckless, *This-is-probably-a-mistake* feeling all mixed up with *Fuck-if-I-care*, and the strange thrill of knowing Jesse was up there in his cabin, right now, with Katie... and *Fuck him*. He wasn't the only one who could get laid tonight.

I grabbed Ash and stopped dead in the middle of the boardwalk.

"Here," I said.

"Here?"

"Yeah." I tugged him against me, and as our bodies connected and I felt him, hard for me, it felt so fucking good.

I was rapidly forgetting that this was a bad, bad idea.

The worst idea.

Friends with benefits?

Did that ever really work?

No. No, I didn't believe it ever really did.

And yet... the words kept coming out of my mouth.

"This is how I want it," I told him. "Right here."

Then I kissed him back, hard.

I fucking devoured him.

I sucked on his tongue, working mine over his, stroking his piercing... rubbing all up on it, on him, as he shoved up my sweater and slid his hand inside my bra. He felt warm in the cold night, his fingers rough with callouses as he squeezed my breast, and I moaned into his mouth. The tingle and the tightening in my nipples was the first rush of true, head-spinning arousal I'd felt in a long, long time.

Then he was working my jeans down over my hips, and my panties, and shoving his hand between my legs.

"You want it slow, Elle?" he asked as he massaged my pussy, slowly, with the palm of his hand, teasing my opening with his fingertips, just lightly. "You want it tender?" He licked his lip. "You want it rough?" Then he delved that magic tongue of his into my mouth again.

The heat and need sparked between my legs, catching fire, and I ground myself into his hand.

"Rough," I choked out between kisses.

Then he pushed me back against the railing. He spread me open and rammed a couple of fingers into me.

I gasped in shock, but I loved it.

"Like this…?" he asked, his voice low with hunger as I undid his jeans and took his cock out. He felt hot and silky in my cold hands.

"Yeah," I gasped, as he fucked me with his fingers, twisting them as he went. He rubbed his thumb over my clit. And it felt *so* good…

Desire was building in me, sharp and quick.

It had been *way* too fucking long…

I squeezed his dick; it was hard and hot. As I worked him in long, tight strokes, I felt the smooth steel ball in the head against my palm. He groaned, and I really didn't care if he came in thirty seconds flat, so long as he got me off.

I wanted it, and I wanted it hard and fast.

"Have you ever… fucked a guy… with a pierced cock?" he asked between kisses, panting for breath.

"No."

He got a wicked smile at that, a very male ego sort of smile. Then he spun me around by my hips. He pushed me forward, bending me over the railing. I heard him rip open the condom packet and felt him roll it onto his dick, his knuckles brushing against me. He held my hips in place with one hand as he lined up his cock with my opening, and I clung to the railing to steady myself.

"Fair warning. It's gonna hit your G-spot and blow your mind."

Yes, please.

But he didn't enter me.

"You good with that?" he asked.

Like any girl wouldn't be good with that?

"Hurry up," I forced out, bracing myself. I'd asked for it rough, and "rough" was probably subjective. "I want it fast."

But he still didn't fuck me.

"Friends, right?" he said.

"Yeah," I breathed, kinda rolling my eyes, though he couldn't see it. "Friends forever."

He smacked my ass. Guess he didn't appreciate the sarcasm, but I didn't mind the spanking, either.

"I'll take the benefits," he said, his voice rough, like it was killing him to hold back. "But I don't want it fucking with the friendship."

"No fucking with the friendship," I said. "Just fucking."

"Okay," he said. "Deal."

Then he thrust into me.

And *hell*, yeah. That feeling; hot, shocking… fucking amazing.

"Shit," he groaned. He smoothed a hand up the curve of my back, beneath my jacket. "Elle… you're so fucking gorgeous…"

"You don't need to talk," I panted out. "Don't talk."

So he didn't.

He just held my hips, tight, and fucked into me with everything he had. He was panting, grunting as he gave it to me. The boardwalk creaked beneath us. The waves crashed on the rocks below. My heart beat in my throat, behind my eyes. And my pussy throbbed, squeezing around him as he rammed into me.

My body grew hot, inside-out, warmth radiating from my core as he worked me. My entire body tingled, growing desperate for release as he rocked my hips to meet his thrusts, back and forth, pulling me onto his dick again and again… shoving me toward my climax, inch by inch. And I wanted him to push me there.

So I let loose, relaxing with an exhale, and just let myself have this. I gave into it, for just this moment.

Because I deserved this, right?

Lucky for me, my friends with benefits was a great fuck.

He knew just what to do, how to give it to me hard, without hurting me in the process. How to hold me with his strong hands. When to grind up against me to hit my clit, and when to almost pull out for a breath or two, just to make me want it more.

He even knew when to release my hips and wrap his arms around me so I could feel his heat, his strain and need and his panting breaths, against me. When I needed that feeling of comfort, of acceptance, to really let go.

And he was right about the piercing.

I could feel this crazy-hot pressure building inside as he stroked me in all the right ways. I was definitely going to come— screaming and totally losing it, like a woman who hadn't come with a man in ten long months.

Who hadn't been fucked, or held, or wanted in this way—up close and intimate—in way too fucking long.

And I realized, somewhere deep in the throes of it, on the very edge of orgasm… that this was *exactly* what I needed right now. Maybe it was what I'd needed all along.

A man who just plain wanted me.

And I didn't care what that want was all about. Dissecting it, inspecting it, rejecting it; as of right now, I was just plain *done* with outright dismissing every man who came along because he wasn't Jesse Mayes.

Jesse Mayes didn't want me.

This man did.

Ash did.

My friend.

Now, my lover.

And getting fucked in the near-dark, in the middle of the night, in the woods, from behind, with my clothes half-on… it was downright feral.

But it wasn't just sex. Not for me.

It was crazy-emotional as I trembled and panted in his arms…

I lay my head back against his shoulder. I reached up behind me and grabbed his hair in fistfuls as he kissed my neck, and I held on tight—as all the shit I'd been holding onto, kept locked down tight, came broiling to the surface. The overwhelming tension of it all. The weight of the heartbreak and loss I'd carried around for the last year of my life like a fucking anvil. The crushing *pressure*.

It all just smashed free.

And I came… gasping into the night with the release. Knowing in that instant, with crystalline clarity, that nothing would ever be the same again.

I also knew that I wasn't exactly thinking about Ash when I came—the gorgeous man embracing me, ramming up against me, inside me, as he shuddered and groaned with his own release.

I was thinking about someone else.

But not in a bad way.

Because this was a new beginning. The beginning of *really* letting Jesse go.

I knew it as I rolled on the waves of orgasm, as another man held me tight in his arms…

This was what letting go felt like.

THE END

Thank you for reading!

Don't miss **Dirty Like Seth**,
the next book in the Dirty series!

Books by Jaine Diamond

**For the most up-to-date list of Jaine Diamond's
published books and reading order please go to**
https://jainediamond.com/books/

Dirty Series

Dirty Like Me

Dirty Like Us

Dirty Like Brody

A Dirty Wedding Night

Dirty Like Seth

Dirty Like Dylan

Dirty Like Jude

Dirty Like Zane

Players Series

Hot Mess

Filthy Beautiful

Sweet Temptation

Lovely Madness

Flames and Flowers

Vancity Villains Series

Handsome Devil

Rebel Heir

Wicked Angel

DEEP Duet

DEEP (DEEP #1)

DEEPER (DEEP #2)

Never miss a book—join Jaine's **Diamond Club Newsletter**

at jainediamond.com to get new release info,

insider updates, giveaways and free bonus content.

Acknowledgments

First off, thank you to everyone who entered the *Name A Dirty Character* contest, which I ran shortly before publication of this book. It was such a fun idea from the outset, and with nearly 500 entries, it was an extremely difficult choice! In the end, Summer was chosen as the winning name—a huge thank-you goes out to Shellcey Germano, who entered the name Summer in the contest! Summer is a new female supporting character, first mentioned in this book (in the fourth story, *A Dirty Deal*); Summer will first make an appearance in the next book, *Dirty Like Seth*, and may also get her own book down the road, if we (and the men of the Dirty world) fall in love with her! (Update: Summer's book is *Sweet Temptation*!) Also, a special thank-you to Linda Fox and Desiree who both entered the name Skye, which was a (very) close runner-up name in the contest.

Thank you, as always, to the many bloggers and reviewers who continue to support me and my books, writing passionate reviews of my new releases simply out of a love for reading and enjoyment of my books. You amaze me and I am deeply grateful. You'll be hearing from me as soon as the next book is ready!

To the ladies in my book club, for throwing my first (awesome!) book signing parties and sharing your passion for books—including the ones I've written. Thank you for making me read to you. Scary but good. ;) To Chris, for hosting and beta reading and being so generous and cool. And to my many other girlfriends, friends and family who continue to support me in my writing and spread the word about my books to other readers—thank you.

To Guinevere, thank you for beta reading and enthusiastically supporting me and loving these stories. How cool is it that you're now an author? Congrats on getting published, lady.

To Mr. Diamond, thank you for beta reading, as always, for helping me make it better, for sharing this dream of mine (ours!) and giving it wings. Love you. Now let's make some more books!

To my readers: THANK YOU for reading this book and for coming along on this journey with me. Your daily messages, kindness and support mean everything to me. To know that my writing has touched your lives is awe-inspiring. Thank you for reaching out to connect with me. I'm humbled by your awesomeness. I'm so honored that you chose to read this collection of love stories; my intent as a romance author is to spread love. As an independent author, I could not do what I do without you. If you've enjoyed this story collection, please consider leaving a review and telling your friends about this book; your support means the world to me.

With love and gratitude,
Jaine

Playlist

Even though this is a collection of stories and not a novel, I had to make a playlist for it. How could I not? Music features so prominently in the lives of these characters, and in my own—including while I was writing this collection.

As usual, some of the songs on the *A Dirty Wedding Night* playlist are mentioned in the stories; others are songs that captured the feel of a certain scene or that I listened to while writing the collection.

The playlist of course features rock—from classic rock to hard rock and everything in-between—as well as other genres that I, and the characters in the book, enjoy as well.

Enjoy the tunes!

*You'll find the links to the full playlists
on Spotify and Apple Music here:*
http://jainediamond.com/a-dirty-wedding-night/

A Dirty Vow

Every Little Thing She Does Is Magic — The Police
No Diggity — Chet Faker
Everlasting Light — The Black Keys
A Sky Full Of Stars — Coldplay

A Dirty Secret

Sex Type Thing — Stone Temple Pilots
Animals — Maroon 5
Fireside — Arctic Monkeys
The Trouble with Us — Marcus Marr & Chet Faker

A Dirty Lie

Closer — Nine Inch Nails
Do I Wanna Know? — Arctic Monkeys
Hey Jude — The Beatles
She's Long Gone — The Black Keys

A Dirty Deal

Emotional Rescue — The Rolling Stones
Snap Out Of It — Arctic Monkeys
You Used to Hold Me — Calvin Harris
No Good — Kaleo

About the Author

Jaine Diamond is a Top 50 Amazon bestselling author of contemporary romance. She writes badass, swoon-worthy heroes endowed with massive hearts, strong heroines armed with sweetness and sass, and explosive, page-turning chemistry.

She lives on the beautiful west coast of Canada with her real-life romantic hero and daughter, where she reads, writes and makes extensive playlists for her books while binge drinking tea.

www.jainediamond.com

Join the readers' group Jaine Diamond's VIPs on Facebook to chat with Jaine and other readers.

Preview of Dirty Like Seth

Don't miss the next full-length novel in the Dirty series, ***Dirty Like Seth***—Seth and Elle's story!

Dirty Like Seth is a reunited-friends-to-lovers redemption story, featuring a fallen hero in need of forgiveness, a superstar heroine who knows how lonely it is at the top, and a secret love that flourishes despite the odds stacked against it.

———

CHAPTER ONE

Seth

I'd done some dangerous shit in my life. Stupid-dangerous shit.

Getting hooked on heroin.

Overdosing.

Almost dying at the age of twenty-two.

Yeah; those were definitely top three.

But this, right now, had to rank right up there on the stupid-dangerous list.

For one thing, I was trespassing on private property, on the lot outside a bar owned by a member of my former band, Dirty. The entire band was inside the bar, and while they had no idea I was here, they were about to find out. And I really wasn't sure how they were going to react.

But no doubt, they probably weren't going to roll out the red carpet for me.

For another thing, the bar was crawling with security, and the security guys who shadowed Dirty these days were mostly of the ex-military or biker variety. Which meant a whole lot of dudes who knew how to draw blood.

And last but not least, I was leaning on a motorcycle parked at the back of the parking lot behind the bar. A Harley. A bike that didn't belong to me but clearly belonged to a serious biker—one of the West Coast Kings, according to the skeletal black King of Spades insignia painted over the gas tank.

It was Jude Grayson's bike. Head of Dirty's security team. At least, I was banking on that being the case.

If it wasn't Jude's, I was banking on, at the very least, that it was the bike of someone he knew, and therefore I was not about to get murdered the instant the biker in question stepped out the back door of the building.

I was doing what I always did when I was nervous: playing guitar. But my mind was on that door. It was painted red, with a security cam on the wall above, pointing straight down. It wasn't pointed at me, but that didn't mean there wasn't some other one that was.

It was early evening and the lot was deserted. There were a few big trucks, the kind that hauled band gear and film equipment and stage shit, and several other vehicles jammed into the narrow parking spaces. But there was a high fence around the lot with a locked gate, and apparently no one in Los Angeles was stupid enough to climb that fence to get in.

No one but me.

I was halfway through Pink Floyd's "Wish You Were Here" when the red door cracked open and some dude's head popped out. He kicked the door wide and stepped outside; he walked right over to me, winding his way through the parked cars as the heavy door swung shut behind him. And yeah, he was a biker. A baby biker. Couldn't be more than nineteen. He had an overstuffed taco in one hand, half-eaten, so I must've interrupted his dinner.

Could've been the dude with the earpiece who'd materialized on the sidewalk shortly after I'd scaled the fence; could've been someone on the security cams. But someone had tipped him off that I was out here. And since it wasn't Jude himself who'd come outside, whoever it was probably didn't recognize me.

Someone new to the team.

This kid, wearing a black leather Kings cut over his T-shirt, a badge stitched to the chest that read *Prospect*, looked more stunned with my idiocy than pissed off. I didn't know him, and whether he recognized me or not seemed beside the point. Either way, his eyes were stabbing out of his head in the direction of my ass, which was resting on the bike seat.

Maybe if I was really lucky he was also stunned by my musical skills, because his eyes kept darting from the bike to my guitar to my face.

"Do you know whose bike that is?" he said, his mouth open and full of taco meat he'd forgotten to finish chewing. Apparently, he was more concerned with my ass trespassing on the bike than with the rest of me in the lot.

I kept playing, looking him steady in the eyes, and said, "I know whose bike it is. You can tell him Todd Becker's here to see him."

The kid shut his mouth, chewed slowly for a bit, and stared at me like he was deciding whether I was dangerous, stupid, or just plain crazy. Apparently landing on the latter, he shook his head. He glanced at the plainclothes security dude on the sidewalk, who was pretending not to eavesdrop. Then he tossed me a biker-brat glare that said *Your funeral* and stalked back inside.

And for the first time today, I actually wondered if this was a giant fucking mistake.

Last thing I wanted to do was get Jude in any kind of shit.

When I first found out about the auditions for Dirty's new rhythm guitarist, I'd planned to head straight up to Vancouver to try out. But then I changed my mind. The auditions were only starting in Vancouver, but ending in L.A. the following week. And the more I thought about it, the more it made sense to wait.

Then I'd called Jude and found out he wasn't even in Vancouver. He was already in L.A.. And that sealed it for me.

I told him I was coming.

He laughed.

Truth was, I didn't think he really believed me.

But here I was.

All week, I'd hung out at the taco dive across the street. Each morning, I watched the lineup of hopefuls grow, winding down the sidewalk behind the velvet rope and around the block. Each afternoon, I watched the crowd dwindle until the last guitarist left the building. Most of the time I'd sat on the sidewalk, playing my acoustic, and even though I wasn't intentionally busking, people had tossed me cash.

That was weird.

I once had a number-one album. Now I had crumpled bills in my guitar case.

The end of each day, I'd bought three tacos and a juice. I'd given them to the old guy who lived out behind the taco place, along with all the leftover cash. Maybe that was just sponsoring an addiction, and maybe after all I'd been through with my own addiction I should've been wary of that. But the dude was seventy-six years old and living in an alley; if he wanted whiskey for breakfast, you asked me, that was his prerogative.

It was several days before I even glimpsed any members of the band.

On Thursday, just as the sun was starting to set, Dylan Cope strode out onto the sidewalk from the gated lot behind the bar—his bar—with a few other guys. The dude was crazy tall, plus his unruly auburn hair was aflame in the evening sun, so there was no mistaking him. He was smiling. Laughing.

Dirty's drummer was definitely the most easygoing of all the band members, and it's not like it had never occurred to me to appeal to his chill nature for forgiveness. Problem was, it would never be that easy. Dylan was a team player almost to a fault; the guy wouldn't change his socks without the approval of the other band members first.

Especially Elle's.

I'd seen her, too, that same evening. Elle Delacroix, Dirty's bassist. Also unmistakable with her long, platinum-blonde hair smoothed back in a high ponytail, her slim, tanned figure poured into a skimpy white dress and tall boots. She'd come outside with a small entourage—her assistant, Joanie, a stiff-looking dude in black who was probably security, and a couple of other women. I didn't even get a look at her face. She'd spoken with the guys, mainly Dylan, and after giving him a hug and a kiss on the cheek, she disappeared behind the building.

Were they dating now? I had no idea.

I wasn't exactly in the loop.

I knew Elle had dated Jesse Mayes, Dirty's lead guitarist, a while back; everyone knew that. So maybe anything was possible. But Dylan remained on the sidewalk with a bunch of guys, talking, some of them smoking, long after the SUV with tinted windows rolled away with Elle.

Today, the very last day of auditions, I'd waited across the street until the end of the day. Until every last one of the hopefuls had been dismissed and wandered away, guitar in hand. I could remember that feeling, vividly. Playing your ass off in hopes of getting noticed, of getting invited back, no idea if that was gonna happen or not.

I'd been in that position several times in my life. None more nerve-racking than when I'd first met Dirty at age nineteen. When their lead singer, Zane Traynor, took me home with him, to his grandma's garage, to meet the band. Once I met them and heard them play, I knew I had to do whatever it took so they'd let me stick around. I'd played with garage bands before. But these guys were something else. And they already had a killer guitarist in Jesse.

So I knew I had to bring something different to the mix.

I spent the next three years of my life hellbent on doing just that.

From that first informal audition, to the last show I ever played as a member of Dirty—the night they fired me from the band—I knew I had to kill it. To work my ass off to earn the chance they'd given me. I had to give them something back that they'd never seen before, never heard… something they couldn't stand to be without.

Just like I had to do now.

And to that end, I'd decided I had to be the very last person they saw today. The last person they *heard*. The very last guitarist to audition for the spot. *My* old spot.

So that no matter what came before, there was no way they could forget my performance in the onslaught of others.

Save the best for last.

That's what I was thinking, what I kept telling myself, as I sat here on the outside, looking in. Just waiting for Jude to come outside and *let* me in.

But I was no stranger to waiting.

I'd waited for seven long years for Dirty to come around, to ask me to rejoin the band. I'd listened to album after album, watched them tour the world, playing my songs, with guitarist after guitarist who wasn't me.

Then that day last year when I saw Zane at the beach… He asked me to come jam with him, just like he did so many years ago. And that jam turned into a meeting with him and Jesse, and that turned into a reunion show in Vancouver, at a dive bar called the Back Door, where we used to play. That was just over six months ago now. Me, up onstage with all four founding members of Dirty—Zane, Jesse, Dylan and Elle—for one song. Our biggest song. "Dirty Like Me."

Then they asked me to come back to the band.

Then Jesse's sister, Jessa, told them some ugly shit about me.

Then they fired me again.

For six months, I waited for a call that never came.

And now here I was. Poised to prove to them all how wrong they were about me, as I played my nerves out with the music. As the red door finally opened… and Jude appeared.

Big, muscular dude. Intimidating, if you didn't know him. Or maybe even if you did. Dark, almost-black hair. Black T-shirt, gnarly tats down his arms, jeans and biker boots.

And one hell of an unimpressed look on his face when he saw me.

He gestured at the plainclothes guy, who was still loitering on the sidewalk, watching me. Just a flick of his chin. *Take a walk*, that gesture said. The dude was gone, around the front of the bar and out of sight by the time Jude stepped out into the parking lot and the door slammed shut behind him.

I'd switched songs, so now I was just trying not to fuck up "The House of the Rising Sun" as Jude stalked over. He stopped two feet from his bike, from me, and looked me over like he was making sure I *hadn't* gone crazy.

"You kiddin' me?" were the first words out of his mouth. They weren't exactly hostile. More like he was mildly stunned, though not as stunned as the kid with the taco.

I stopped playing, flattening my hand over the strings to silence them. "You rode your bike here from Vancouver," I observed. "Took a few days off?"

He crossed his massive arms over his chest. "Like to do that sometimes. Hit the road. Alone. Tune out all the bullshit." He raked his dark gaze over me again. "You bringin' me bullshit?"

"Guess that depends," I said, "how you look at it."

"From where I'm looking, it looks like bullshit."

"No bullshit. This is an audition." I played a few lines from Jimi Hendrix's "Voodoo Child." Showing off, maybe. "I'm here to audition."

Jude still looked unimpressed as shit. "Auditions are closed. Invitation-only. Pre-screened. And I never saw your name on the list... *Todd Becker.*"

"So screen me now," I said, still playing, quietly, as we spoke. "What do you wanna hear? 'Fortunate Son'...? 'Roadhouse Blues'...?" I played a little from each song as I spoke. "'Dirty Like Me'...?"

Jude remained silent, arms crossed, dark eyes watching me as I played. The dude was tough to read, but the Jude I knew had always liked listening to me play.

We'd established a game, early in our friendship, where he'd toss a song title at me and I'd play it for him. If I didn't know the song, no matter what it was, I'd learn it, quick. It was because of Jude and this little game of ours, in part, that I'd become as good as I had on guitar. Because if I ever struggled to master a song he'd requested, he never let me hear the end of it—no matter that the guy couldn't strum out a tune to save his life. And he'd made it a favorite pastime to challenge me with the hardest songs. In some cases, songs I never would've learned if it weren't for him egging me on.

"You still into Metallica?" I started playing "Master of Puppets." Not my favorite band, but back in the day, I'd mastered "Master"—no easy task—to entertain him.

He cocked a dark eyebrow at me, so maybe we were getting somewhere. "You remember it."

"Hard to forget. My fingers actually bled learning it."

He grunted a little at that, which was about the closest I was gonna get to a smile right now. I knew that.

"Or how about some Rage?" I switched to "Killing In the Name" by Rage Against the Machine, another of Jude's favorites. At least it was, years ago.

He shook his head, which I took to mean his admiration of my guitar skills was neither here nor there at the moment. So I did what I knew how to do: I kept playing. My talent was the only real card I had to play here.

Maybe it was the only card I'd ever had to play.

"Killing" was another hard song—both heavy and difficult to master. I'd mastered it. I'd played it for him enough times, long ago, that it was in my blood. Any song I'd ever learned was in my blood; once I'd learned it, good or bad, I'd never lost a song. Even when I was fucked out of my tree on whatever junk I was on. Which was probably how I'd lasted as long as I had with Dirty.

Yes, I'd OD'd on the tour bus and almost died. But I could always get onstage at show time and nail any song.

Jude just stood there, that impassive look on his face; a look perfected over many years working security for Dirty and riding with an outlaw motorcycle club. But since he hadn't yet told me to take a hike, I knew what he was probably thinking.

It wasn't so much that he was considering his own ass—how

this might play out for him if he let me into that bar. More likely he was considering how badly *my* ass was gonna get kicked.

"You want me to dance for you, too?" I challenged, allowing a little sarcasm into my tone.

Jude remained silent until I ran out of song. Then he said, "So this is how it's gonna be, huh?"

"Looks like it."

"Looks like an idiot playing guitar in a parking lot," he said. But then he uncrossed his arms with a small, inaudible sigh. He was looking me over again, top to bottom, seeming to contemplate how quickly the band was gonna recognize me.

I knew the auditions were blind. But it's not like I was hiding who I was. Other than the assumed name, I was still me.

I'd cut off my hair as soon as I arrived in L.A.; it was fucking hot, but the truth was, I was hungry for a change. A fresh start, maybe. No one had seen me with shortish hair since I was twelve, so that was different. I also had a short beard, but I'd been rocking a beard, on and off, for the past few years, and Dirty had seen me bearded. I had aviators on, but this wasn't exactly a glasses on / glasses off Superman trick. I wasn't masquerading as Clark Kent and planning to whip out my cape later.

This was just me.

Faded Cream T-shirt, worn jeans, snakeskin boots, bandana in my back pocket. Metal bracelet with the word BADASS stamped into it, which Elle had given me when I first joined Dirty and I'd never stopped wearing.

They'd see me a mile away and know who I was.

Seth Brothers.

Former rhythm guitarist and songwriter with Dirty. Fallen star. Pariah. And still, whether Dirty liked it or not, fan favorite. No guitarist who'd come after me was loved as much as I was. No one wanted me back in this band more than the fans. I knew that much from the messages I still received on a daily basis. It was the only reason I kept a Twitter account.

It was a big part of what was keeping me here, in the face of increasingly-bad odds. I was starting to feel how bad those odds were, given Jude's hesitation to even let me in the door.

I wasn't quite sure what to do about it. I'd never expected Jude to be my problem.

"You sure you want this?" he asked me, his dark eyes locked steady on mine. "Now?"

"You once said you'd have my back, when the time came."

"I say a lot of shit," he admitted. "Not all of it smart."

"Then we have that in common."

He grunted again. "Tell you what. You play Metallica for me, you've got your audition."

"Great," I said.

Not great. The only Metallica song I knew well enough to impress anyone—maybe—was "Master of Puppets," and that did not feel like the way to go with a Dirty audition. Dirty was not a metal band.

Clearly, that wasn't Jude's problem. He turned his back on me, a non-verbal dismissal, and headed back toward the bar.

I blew out a breath; kinda felt like I'd been holding it all fucking week.

I stuffed my acoustic into its case and picked it up, along with the other case, the one that held my electric guitar—my favorite Gibson. Then I fell in behind Jude.

It wasn't exactly a red carpet, but it would do.

Made in the USA
Monee, IL
27 July 2023